W9-BQF-411

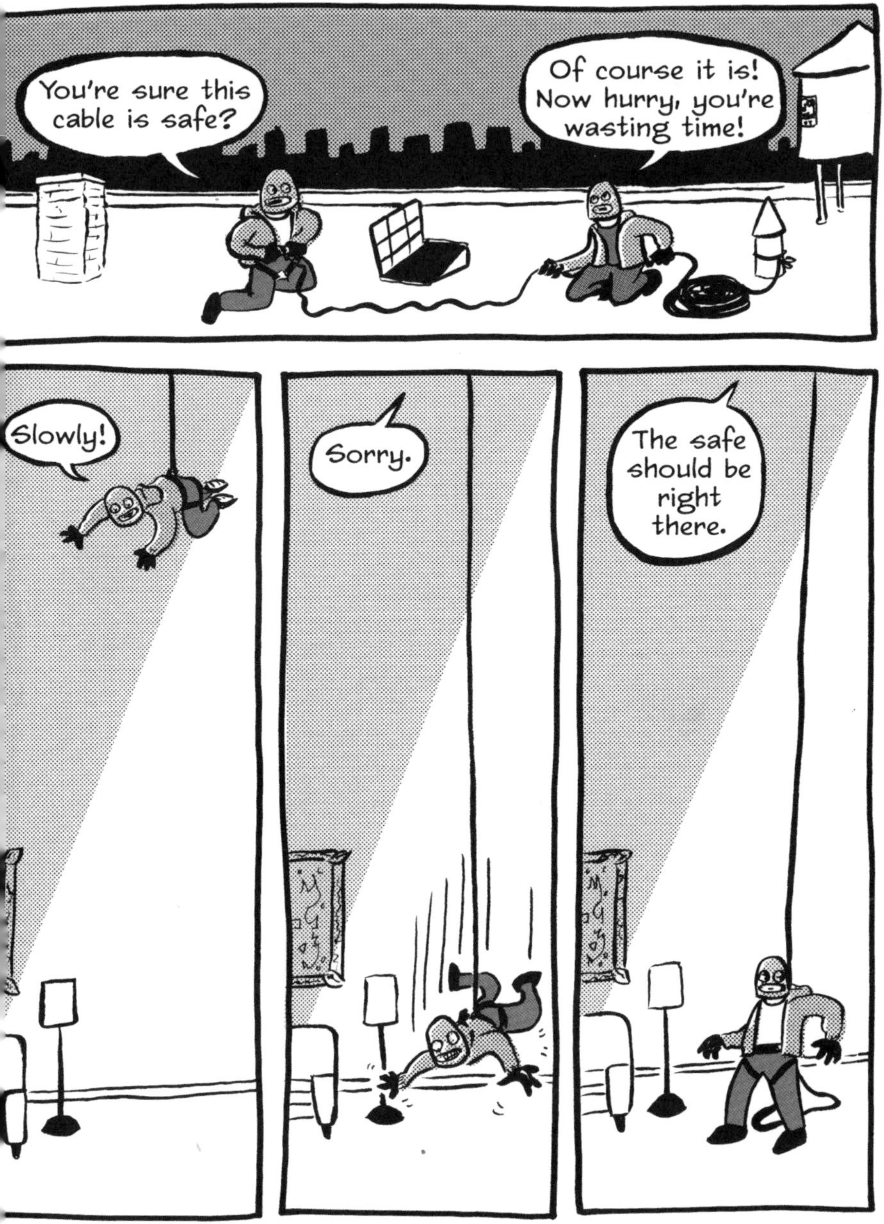
You're sure this cable is safe?
Of course it is! Now hurry, you're wasting time!
Slowly!
Sorry.
The safe should be right there.

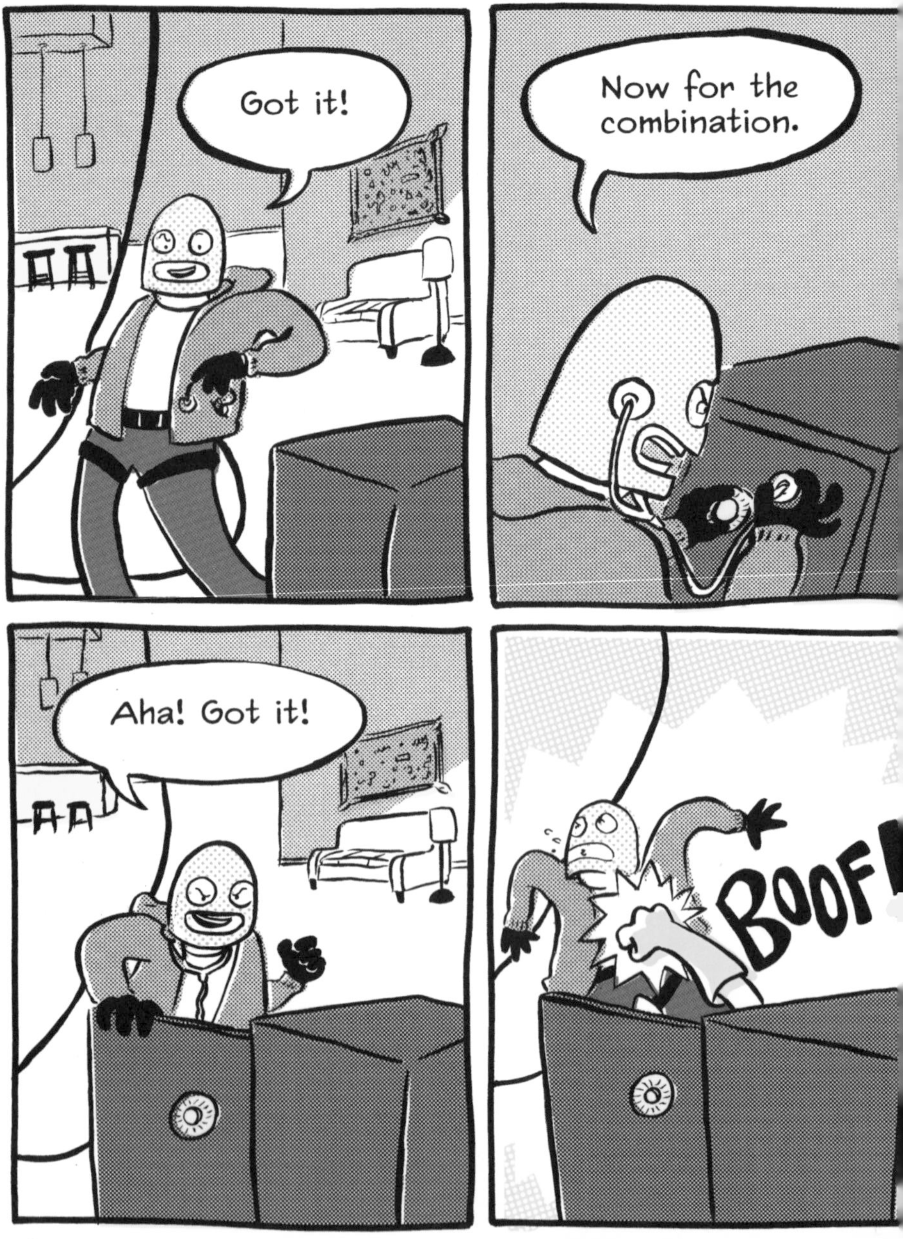
Got it!
Now for the combination.
Aha! Got it!
BOOF

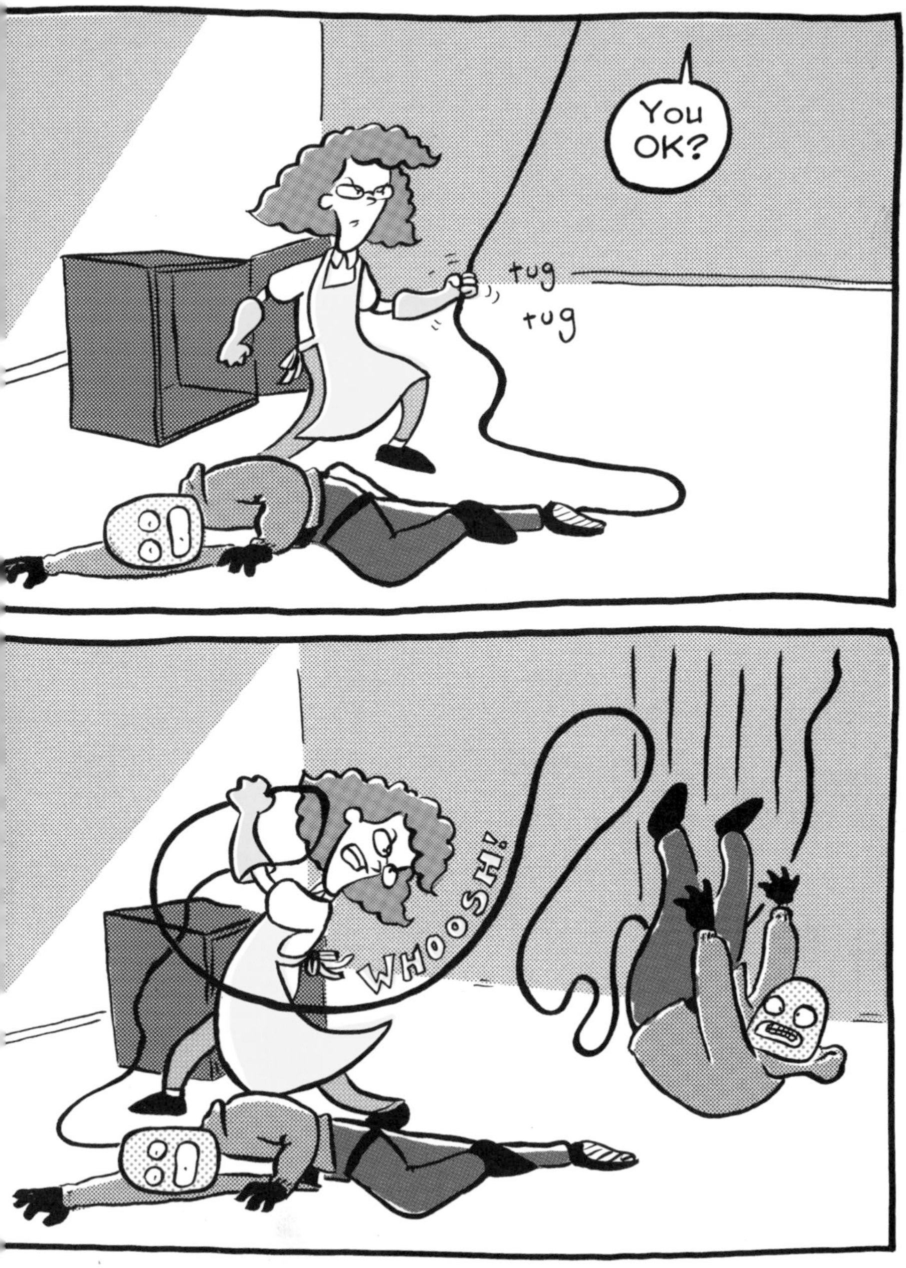
You OK?
tug
tug
WHOOSH!

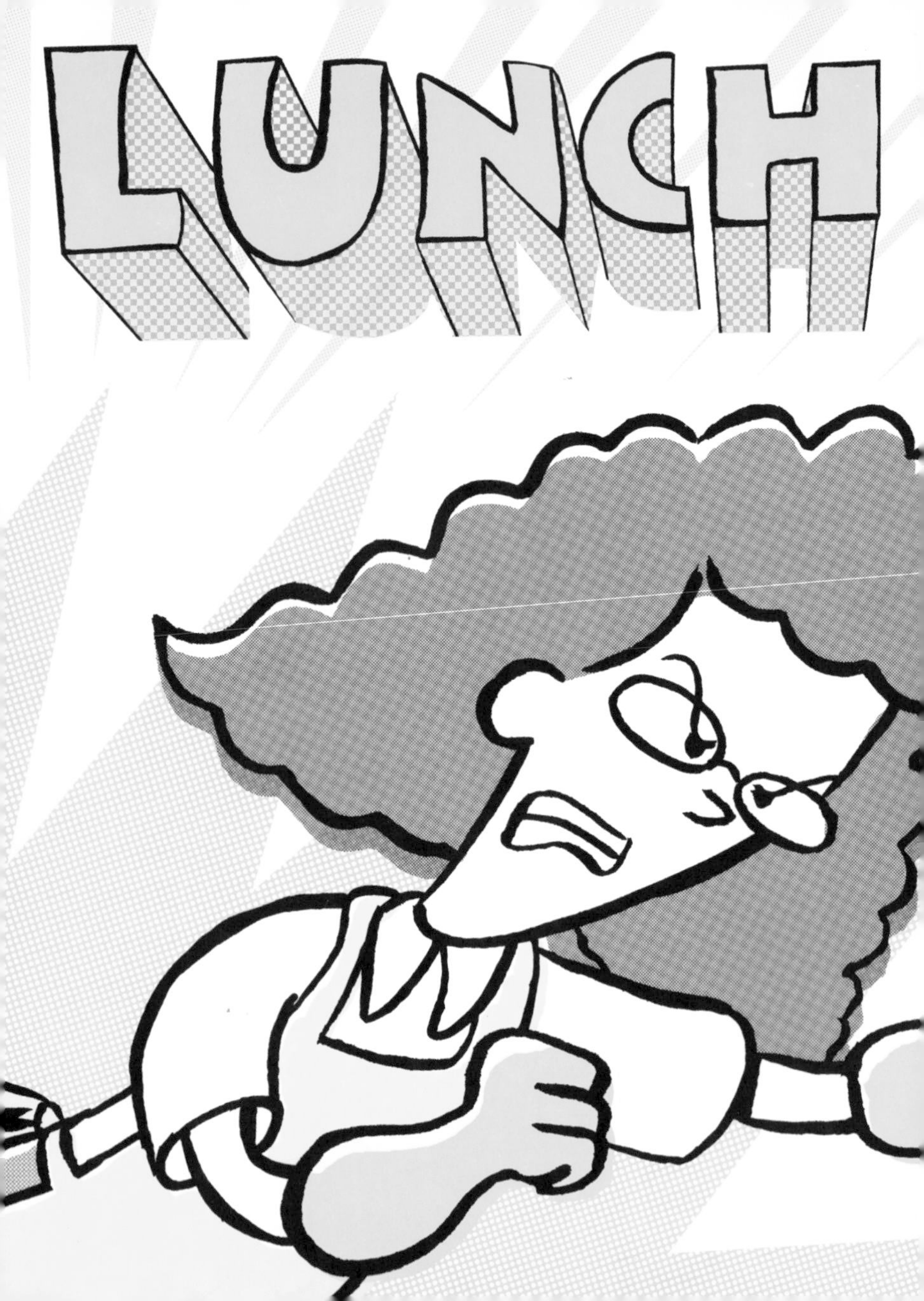
LUNCH

LADY

and the Bake Sale Bandit

Jarrett J. Krosoczka

Alfred A. Knopf New York

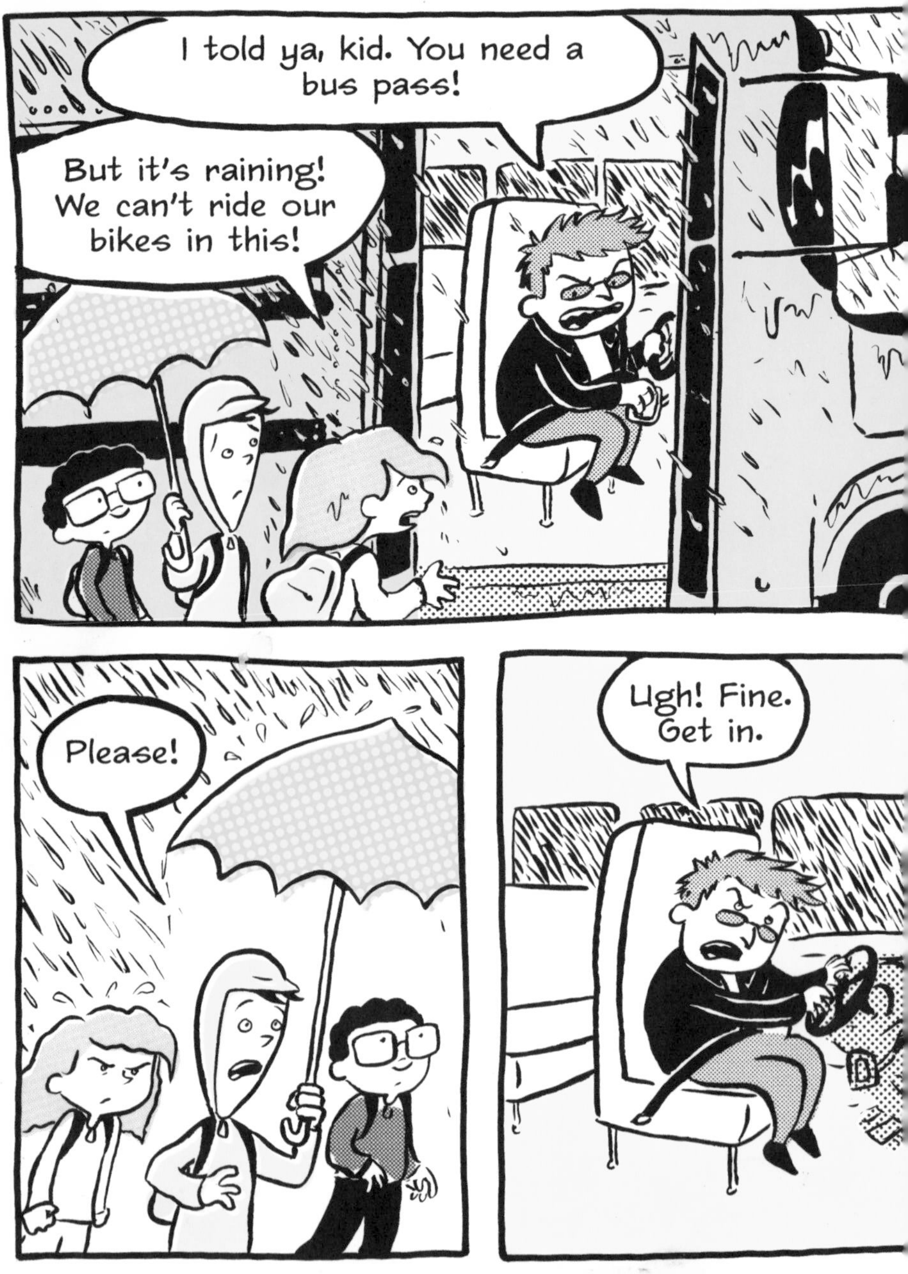
I told ya, kid. You need a bus pass!
But it's raining! We can't ride our bikes in this!
Please!
Ugh! Fine. Get in.

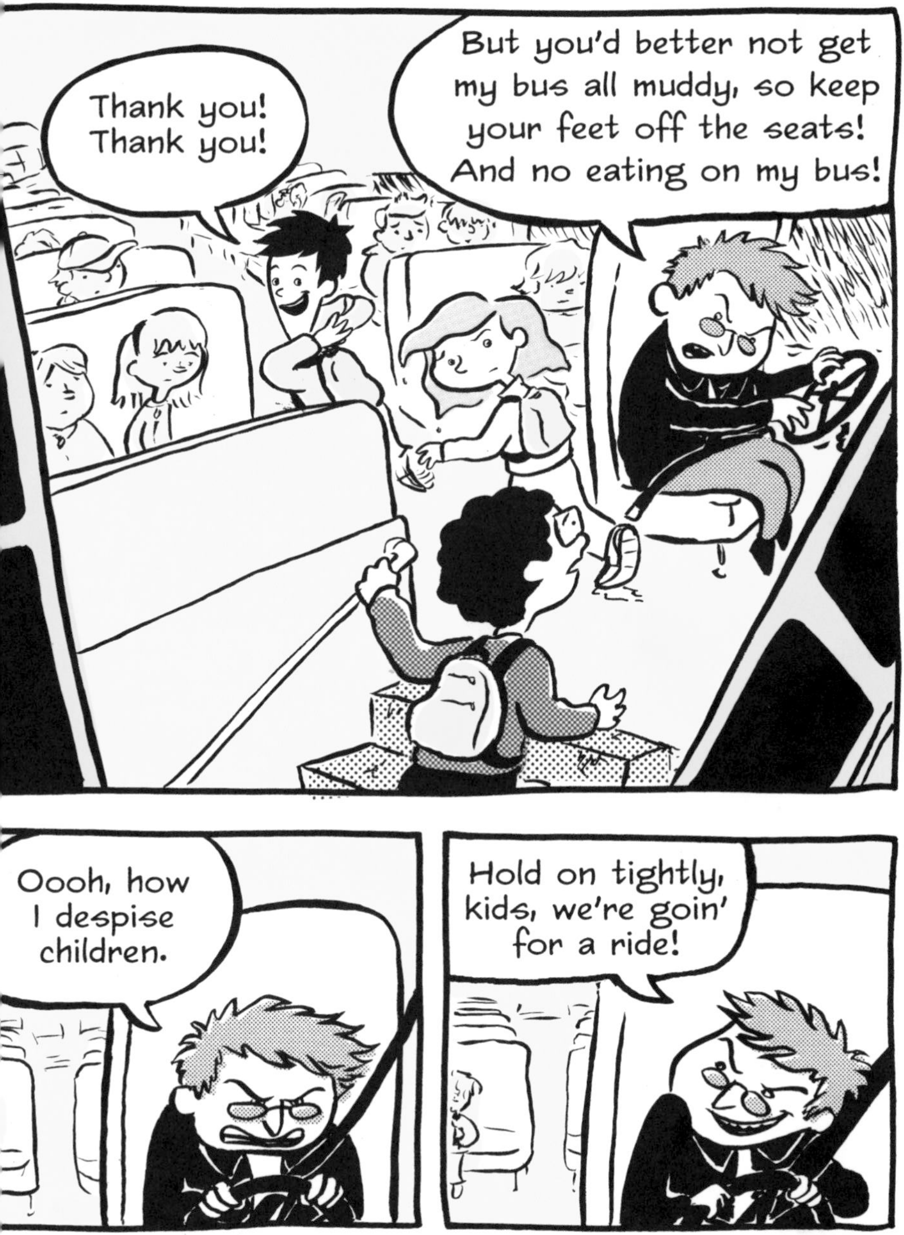
Thank you! Thank you!
But you'd better not get my bus all muddy, so keep your feet off the seats! And no eating on my bus!
Oooh, how I despise children.
Hold on tightly, kids, we're goin' for a ride!

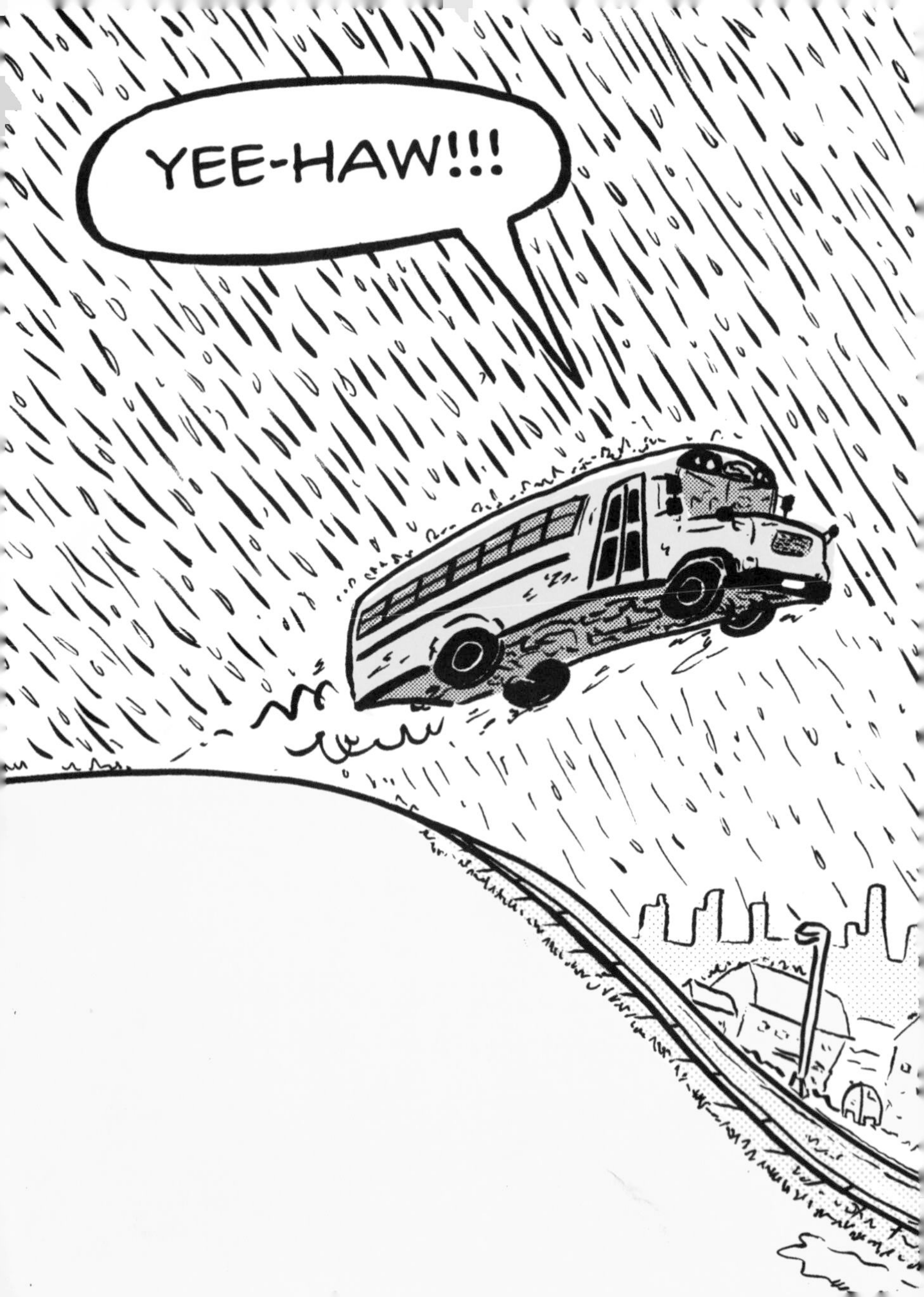
YEE-HAW!!!

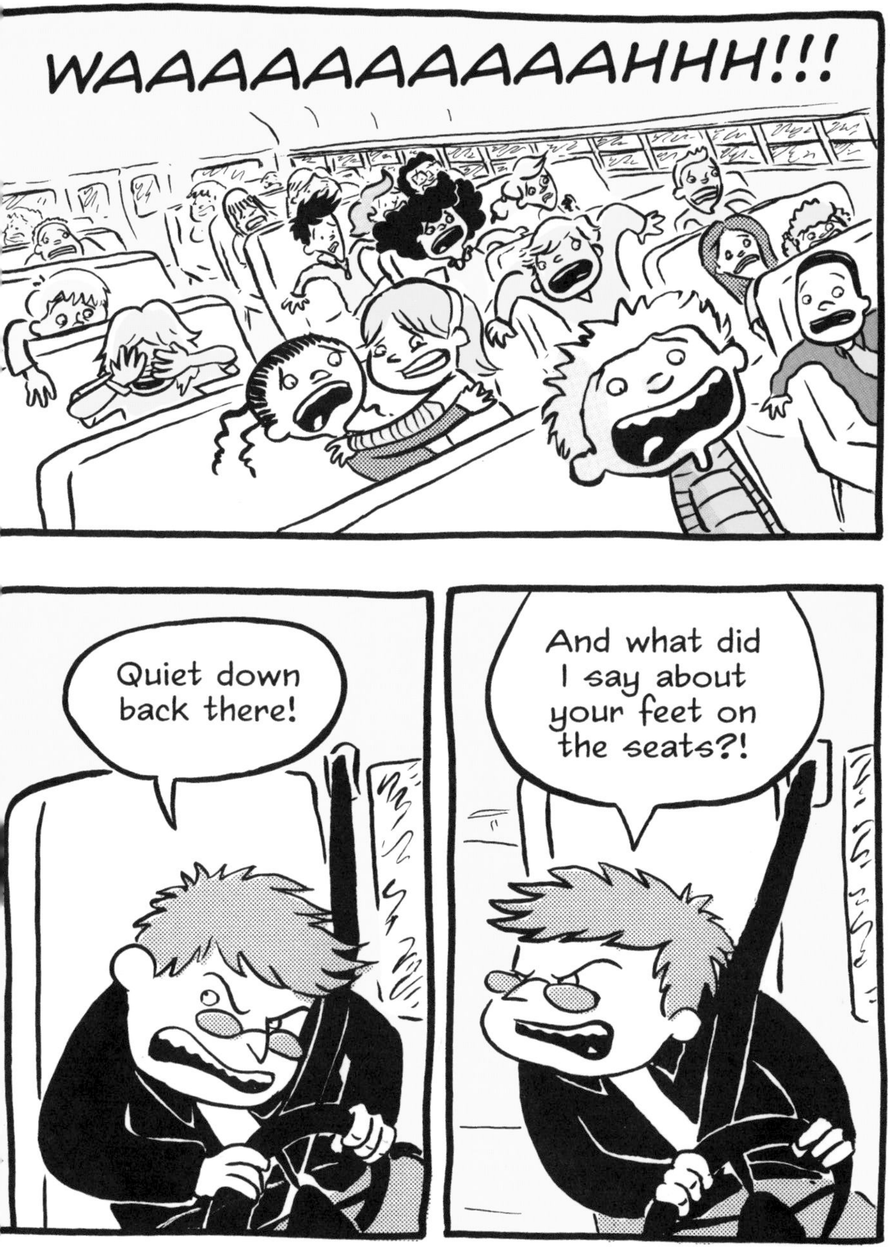
WAAAAAAAAAAHHH!!!
Quiet down back there!
And what did I say about your feet on the seats?!

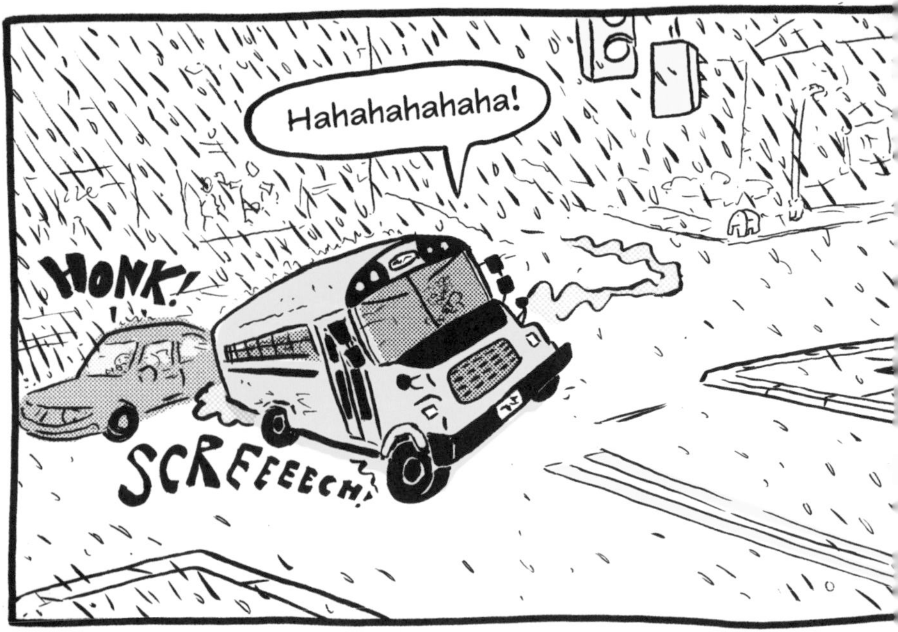
Hahahahahaha!
HONK!
SCREEEEECH!
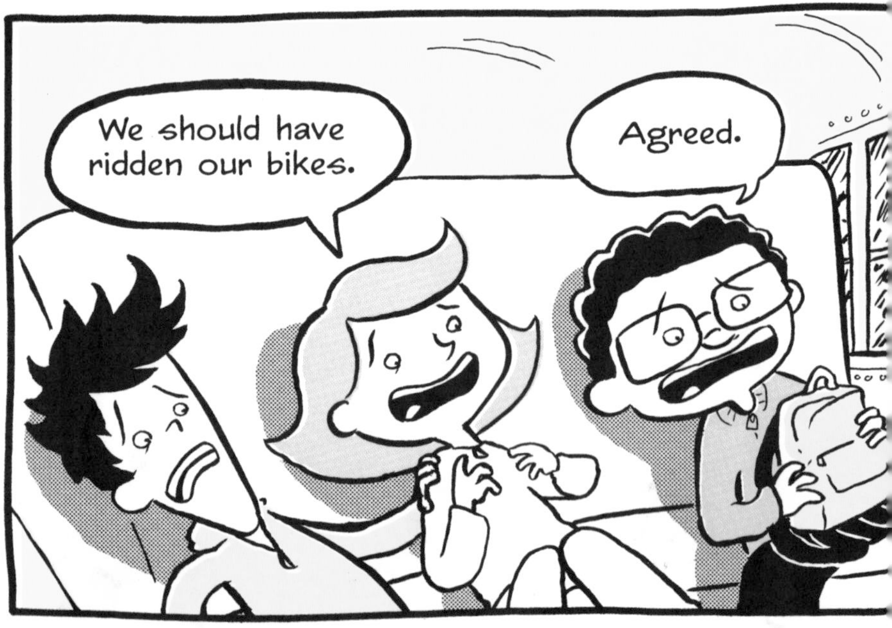
We should have ridden our bikes.
Agreed.

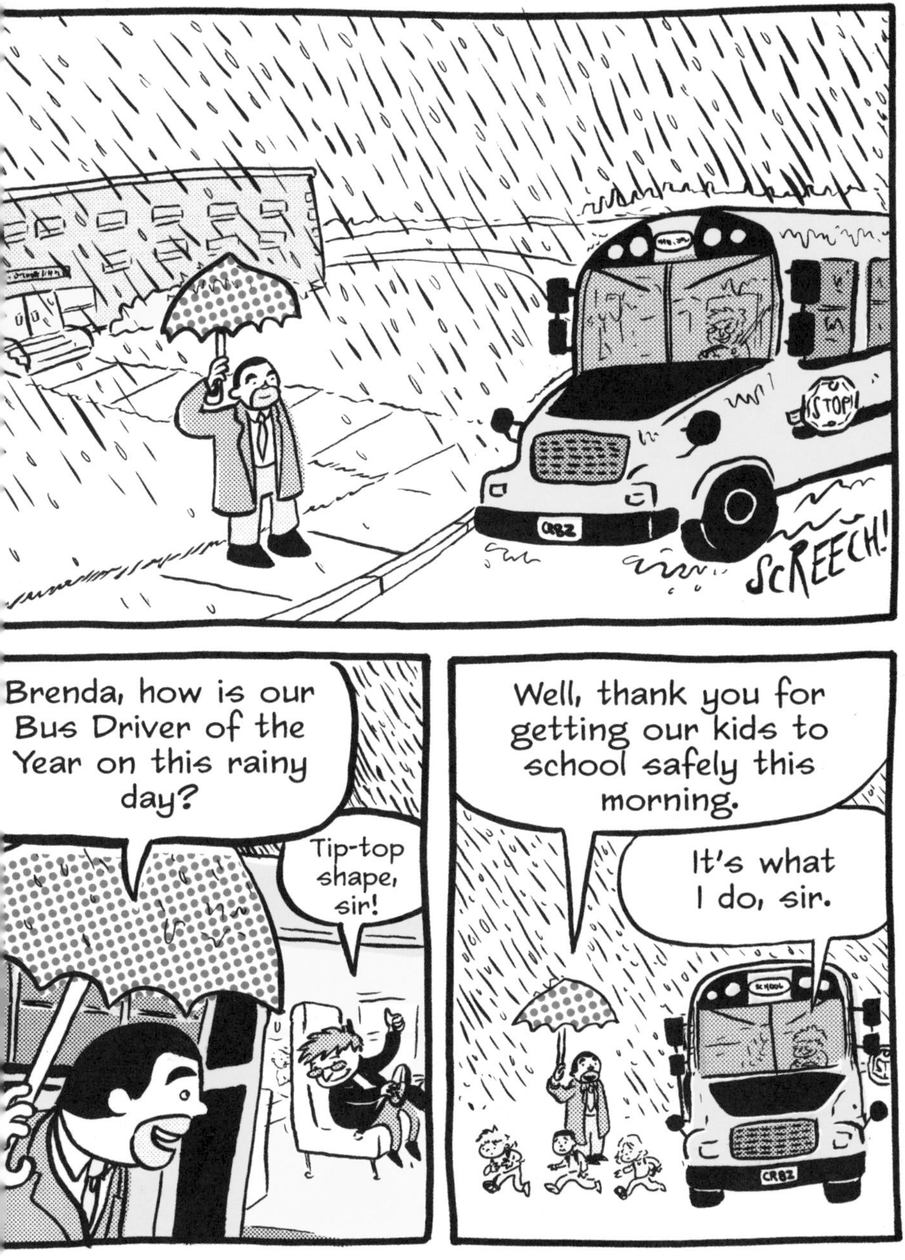
STOP!
CR8Z
SCREECH!
Brenda, how is our Bus Driver of the Year on this rainy day?
Tip-top shape, sir!
Well, thank you for getting our kids to school safely this morning.
It's what I do, sir.
CR8Z

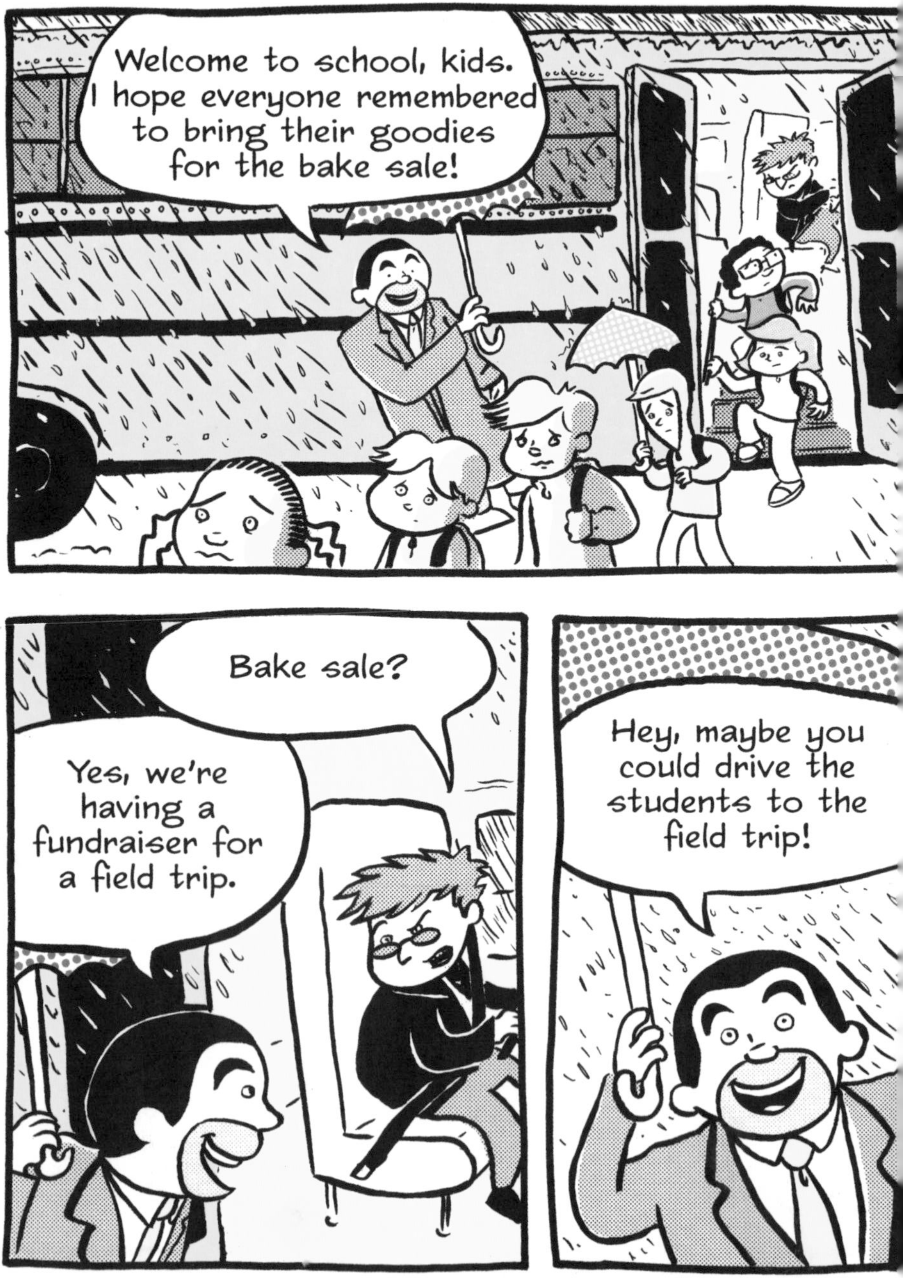
Welcome to school, kids. I hope everyone remembered to bring their goodies for the bake sale!
Bake sale?
Yes, we're having a fundraiser for a field trip.
Hey, maybe you could drive the students to the field trip!

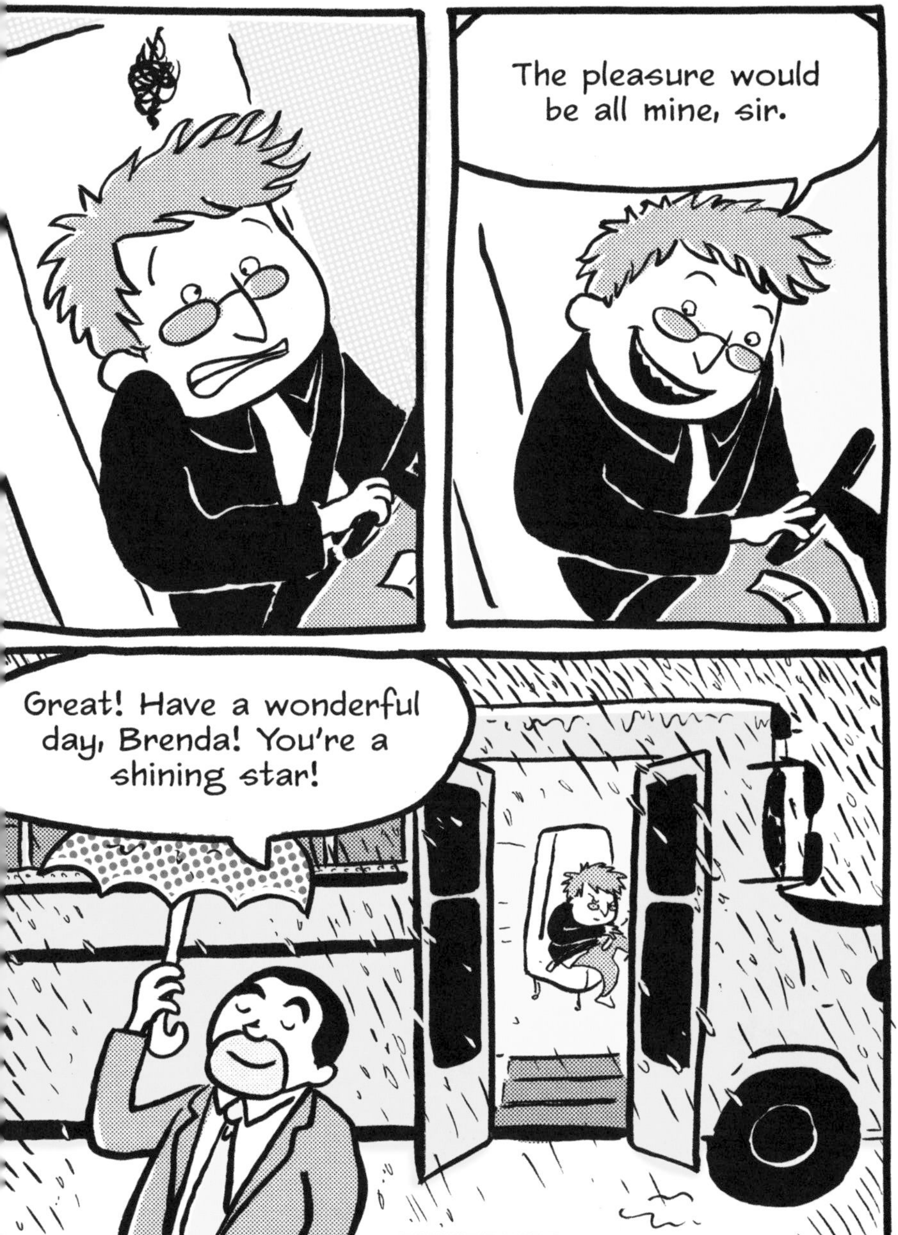
The pleasure would be all mine, sir.
Great! Have a wonderful day, Brenda! You're a shining star!

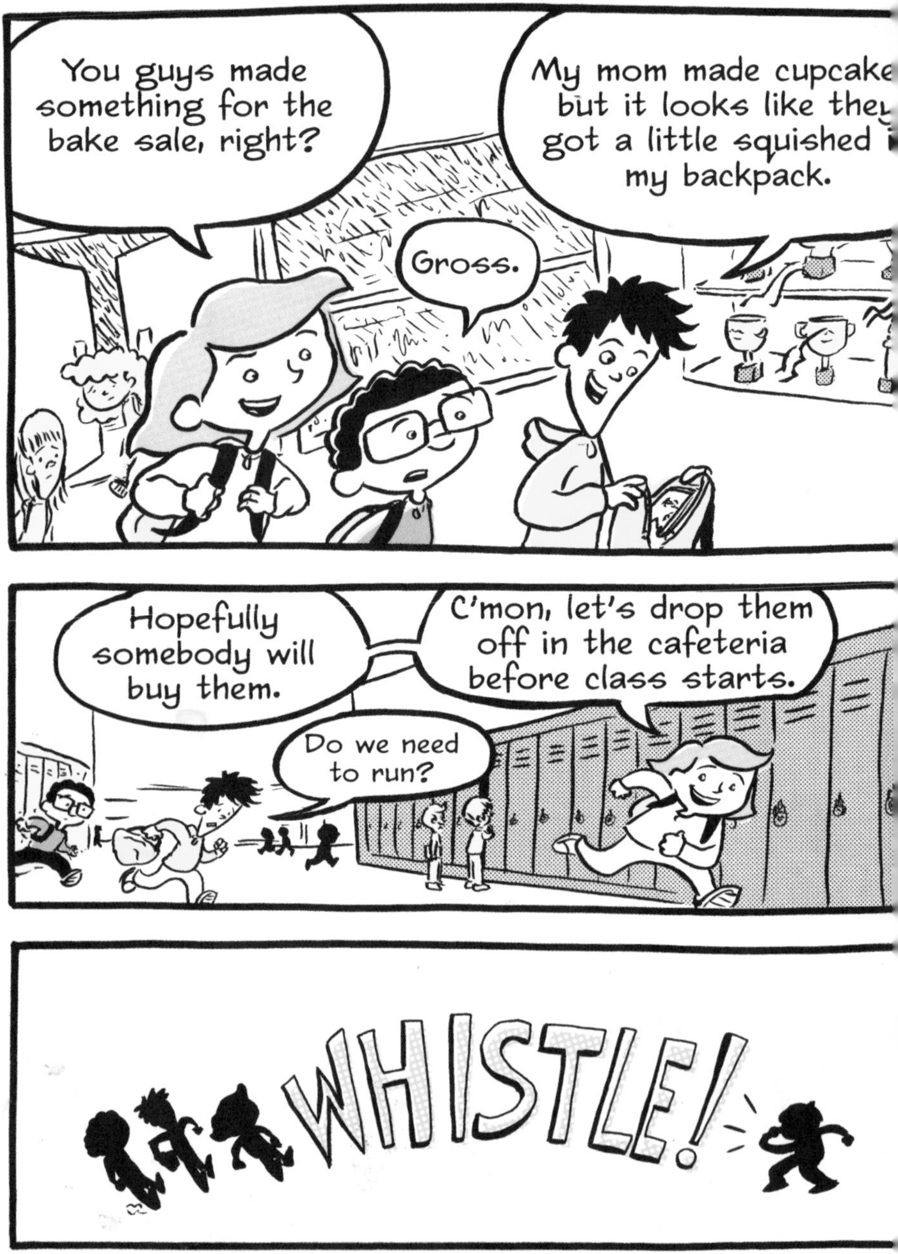
You guys made something for the bake sale, right?
My mom made cupcake but it looks like they got a little squished i my backpack.
Gross.
Hopefully somebody will buy them.
C'mon, let's drop them off in the cafeteria before class starts.
Do we need to run?
WHISTLE!

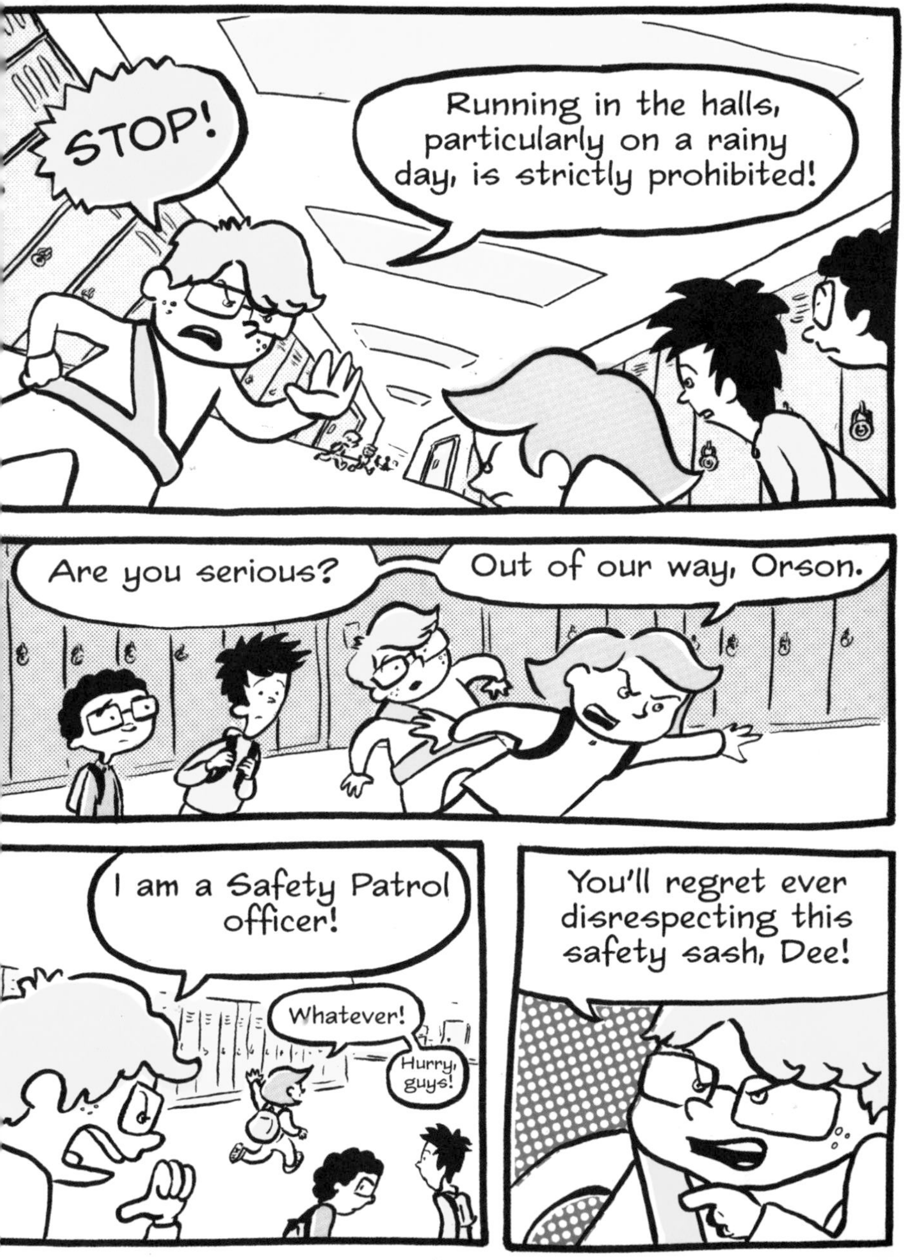
STOP!
Running in the halls, particularly on a rainy day, is strictly prohibited!
Are you serious?
Out of our way, Orson.
I am a Safety Patrol officer!
Whatever!
Hurry, guys!
You'll regret ever disrespecting this safety sash, Dee!

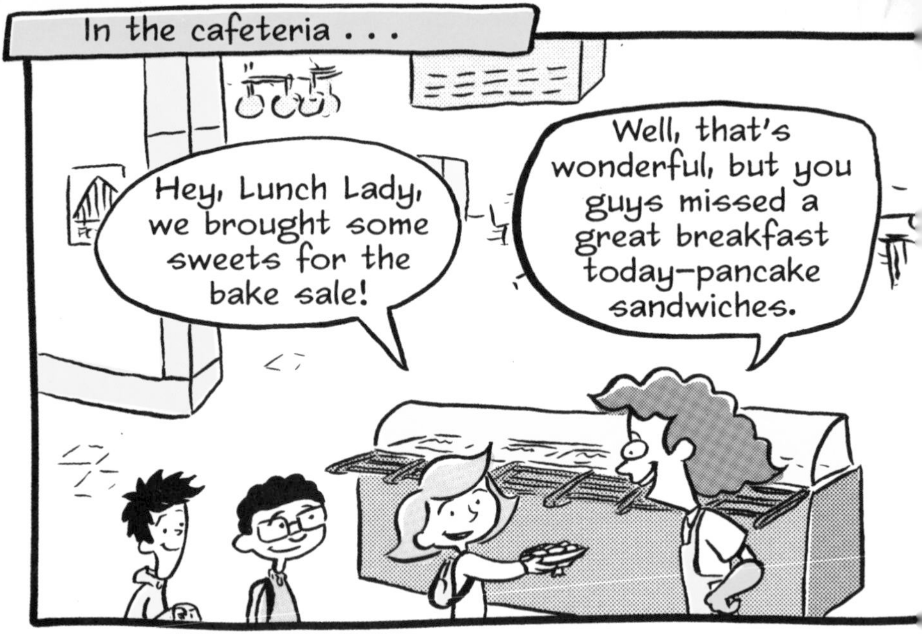
In the cafeteria . . .
Hey, Lunch Lady, we brought some sweets for the bake sale!
Well, that's wonderful, but you guys missed a great breakfast today—pancake sandwiches.

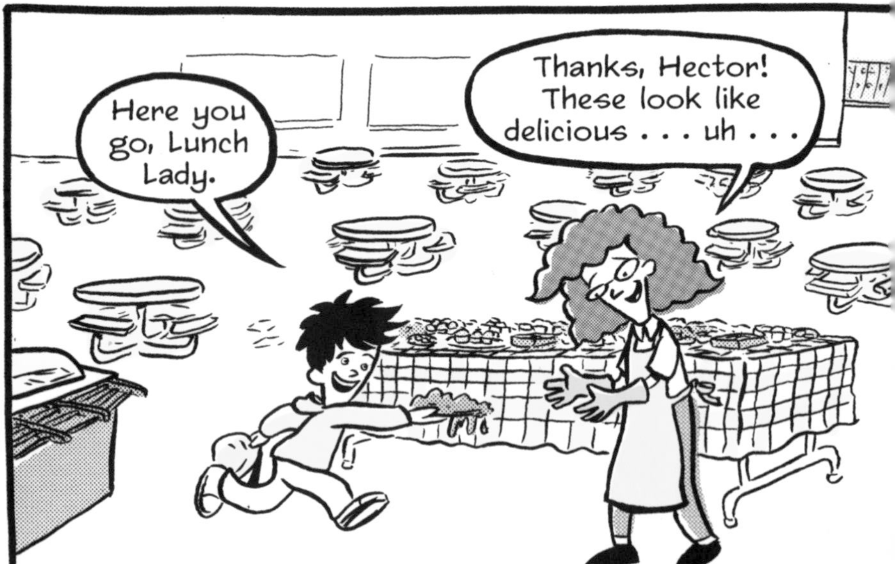
Here you go, Lunch Lady.
Thanks, Hector! These look like delicious . . . uh . . .

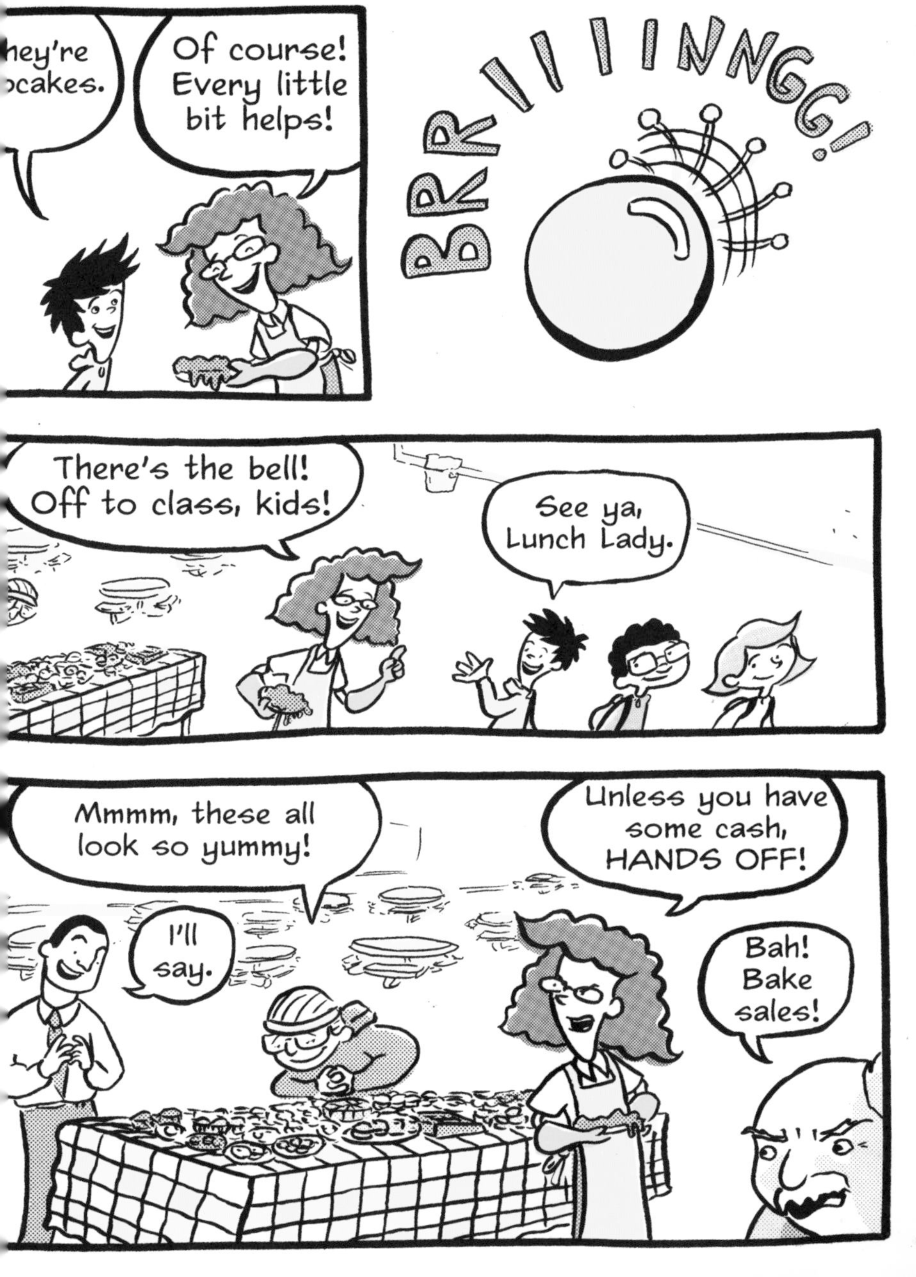

hey're
ocakes.
Of course! Every little bit helps!
BRRIIIINNGG!
There's the bell! Off to class, kids!
See ya, Lunch Lady.
Mmmm, these all look so yummy!
I'll say.
Unless you have some cash, HANDS OFF!
Bah! Bake sales!

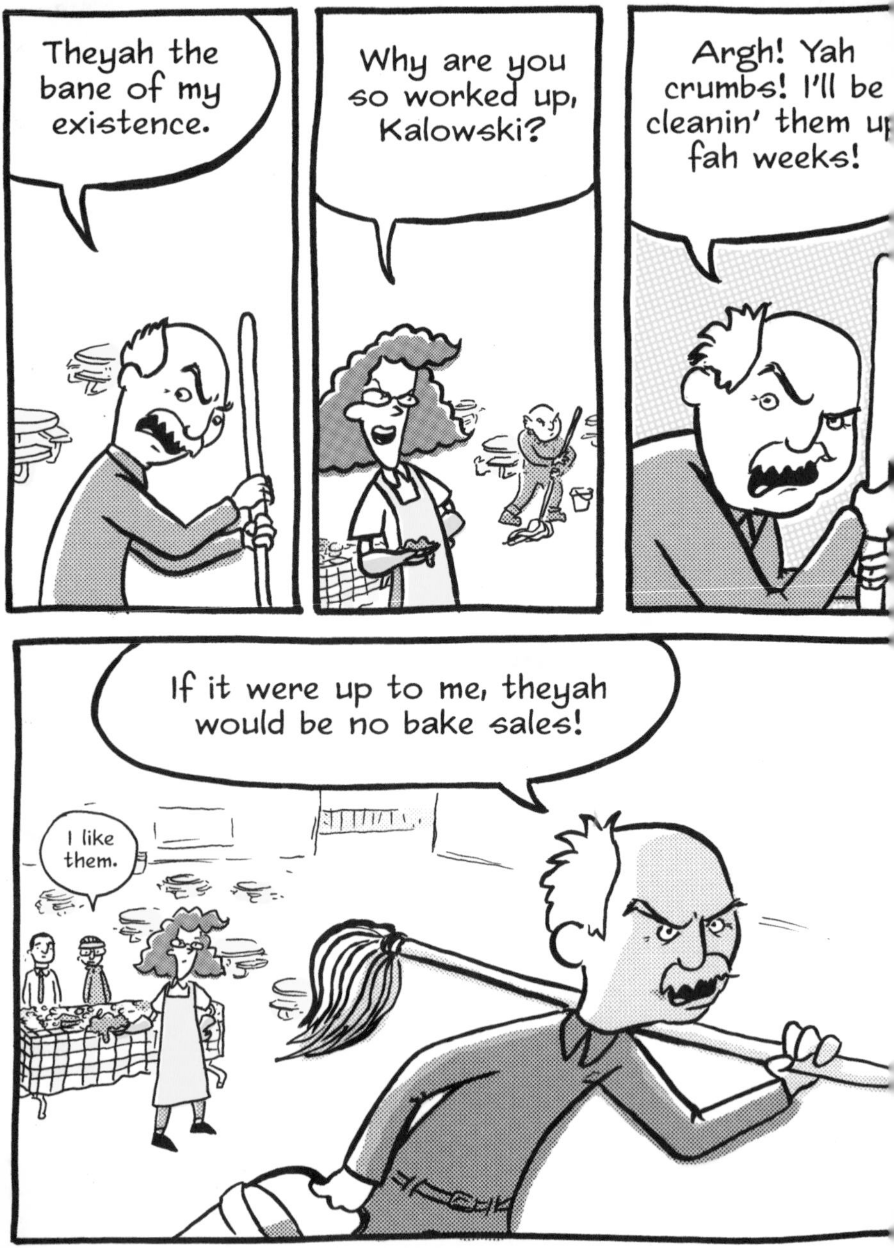
Theyah the bane of my existence.
Why are you so worked up, Kalowski?
Argh! Yah crumbs! I'll be cleanin' them u fah weeks!
If it were up to me, theyah would be no bake sales!
I like them.

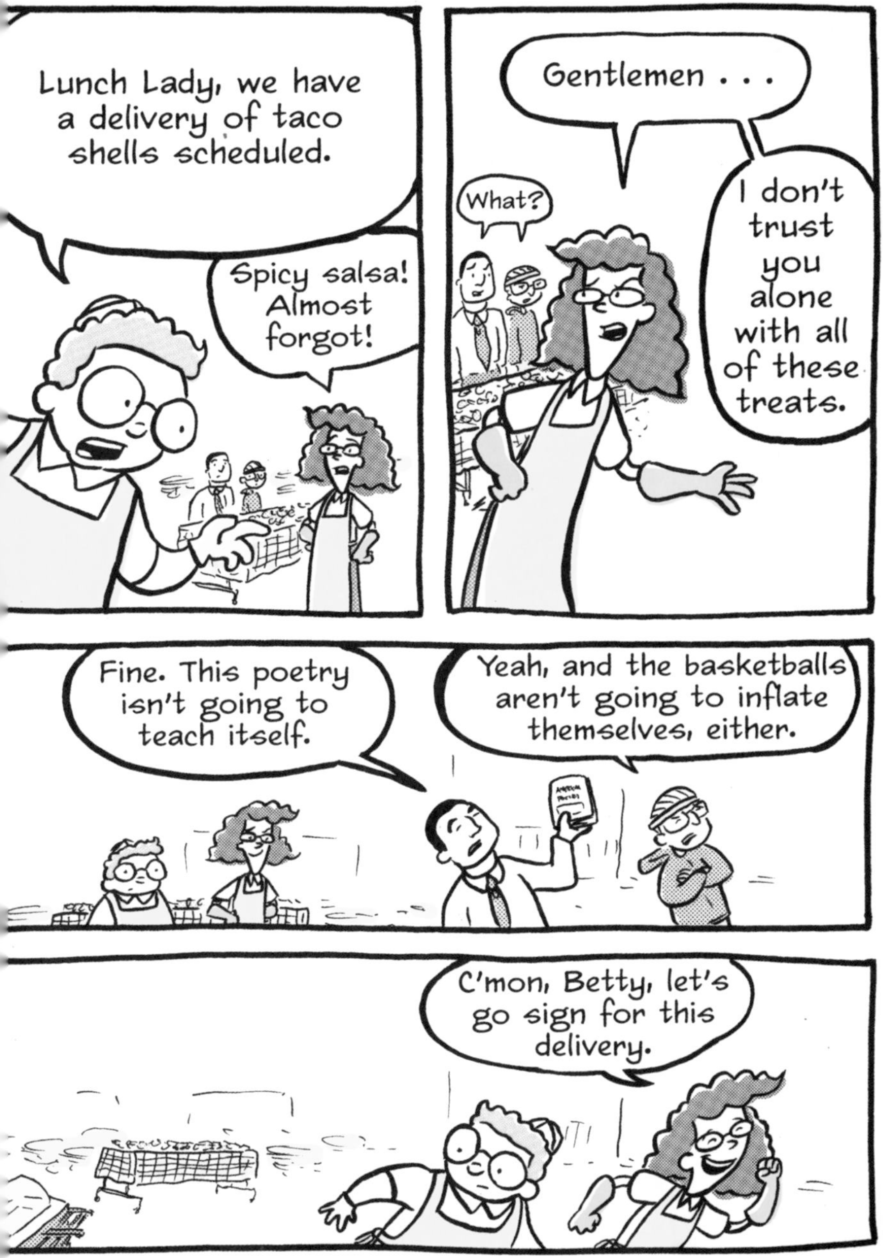
Lunch Lady, we have a delivery of taco shells scheduled.
Spicy salsa! Almost forgot!
Gentlemen . . .
What?
I don't trust you alone with all of these treats.
Fine. This poetry isn't going to teach itself.
Yeah, and the basketballs aren't going to inflate themselves, either.
C'mon, Betty, let's go sign for this delivery.

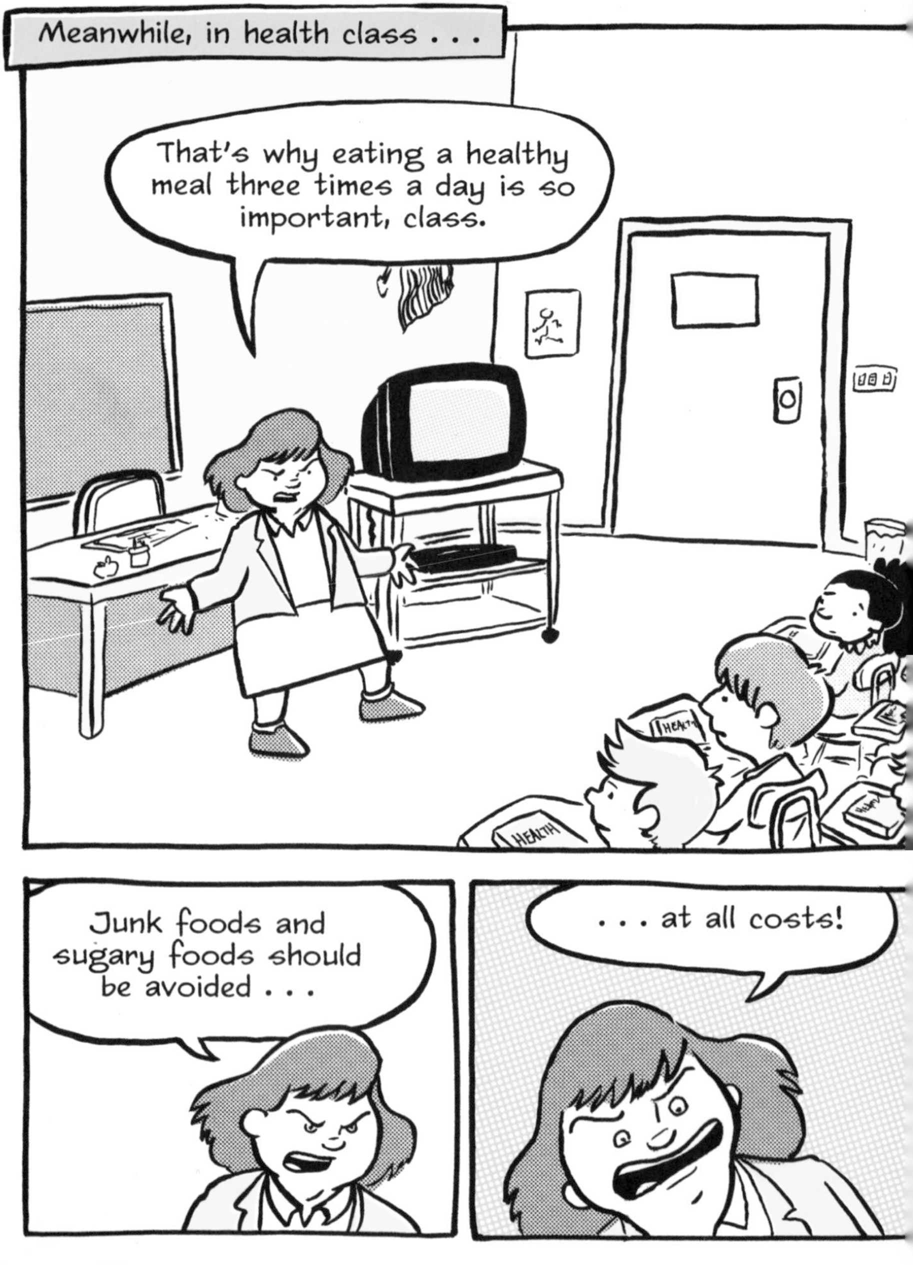
Meanwhile, in health class . . .
That's why eating a healthy meal three times a day is so important, class.
HEALTH
HEALTH
Junk foods and sugary foods should be avoided . . .
. . . at all costs!

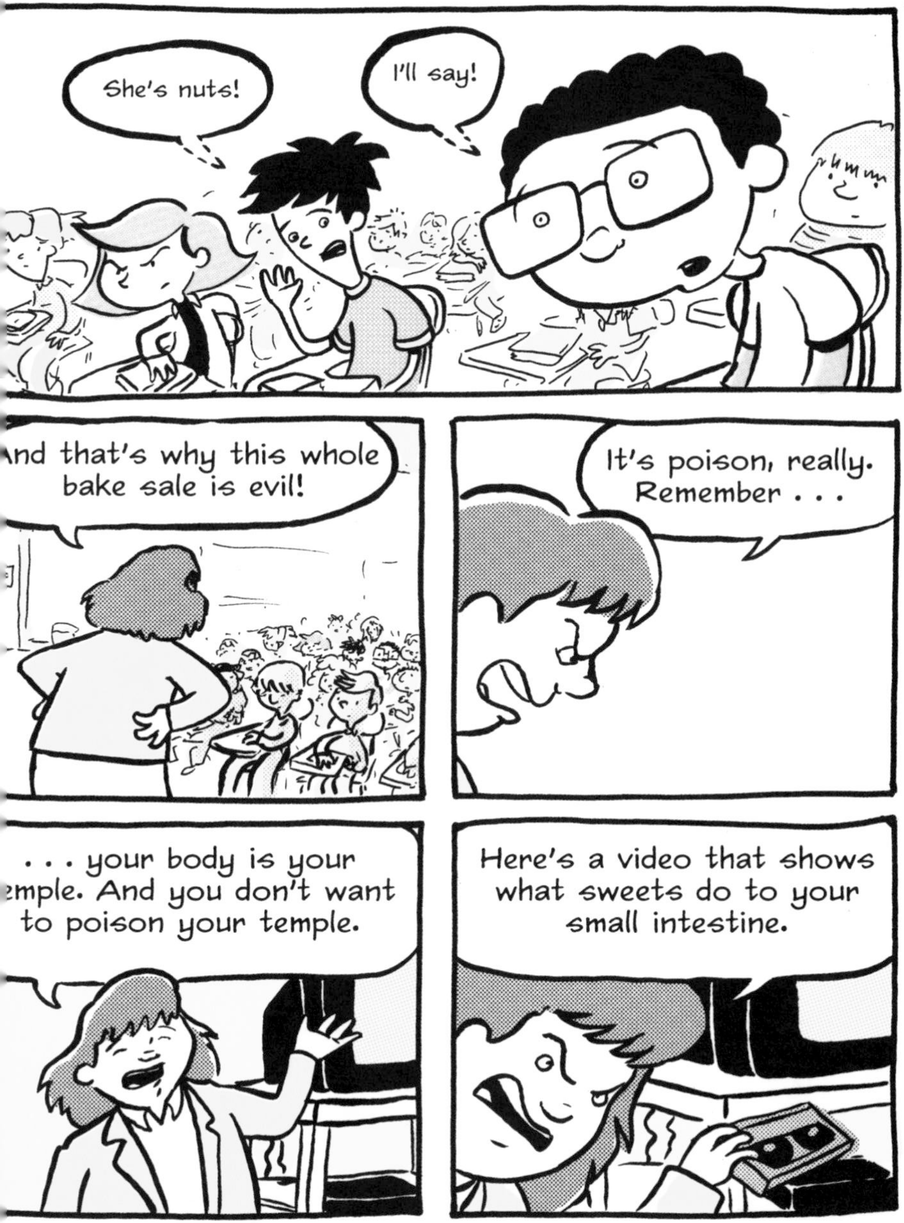
She's nuts!
I'll say!
And that's why this whole bake sale is evil!
It's poison, really. Remember . . .
. . . your body is your temple. And you don't want to poison your temple.
Here's a video that shows what sweets do to your small intestine.

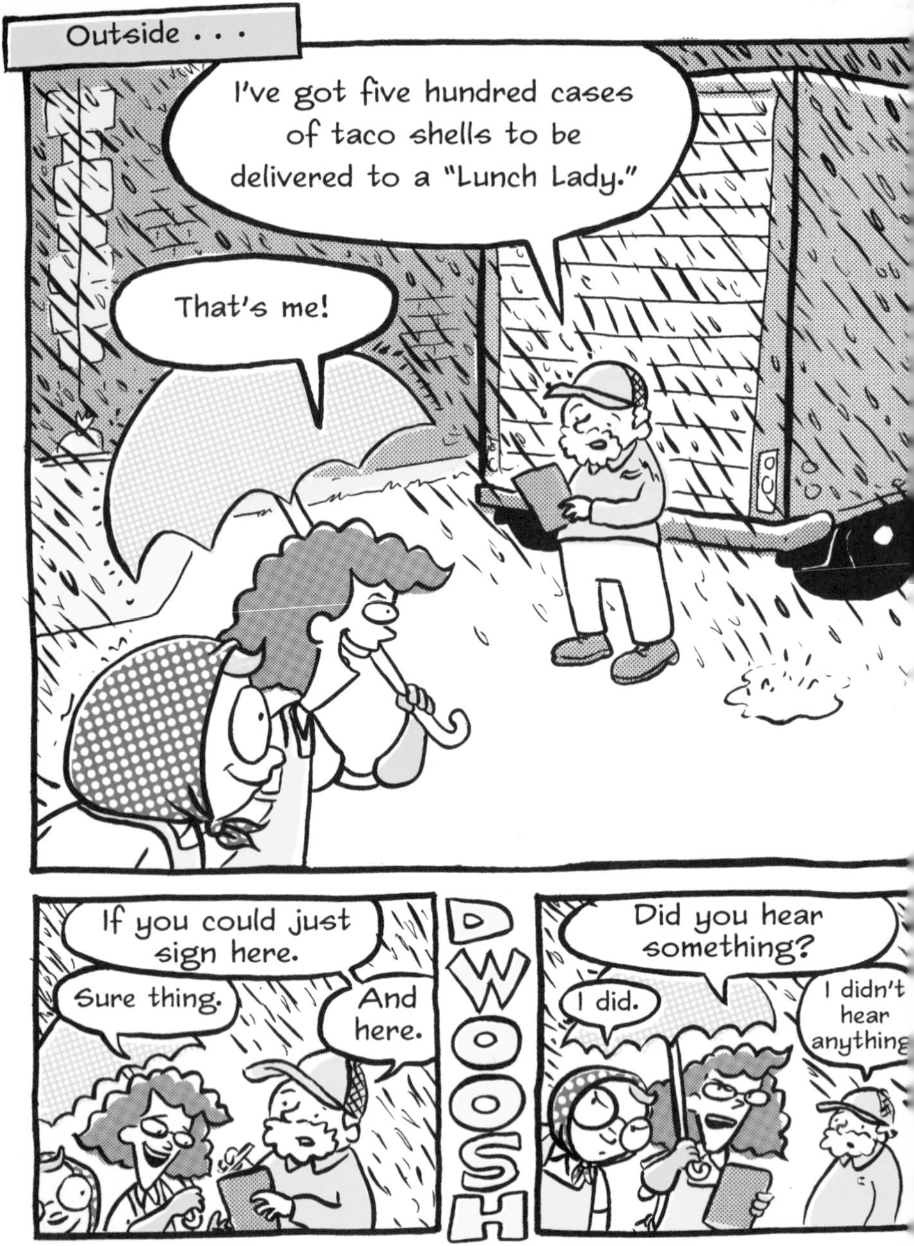
Outside . . .
I've got five hundred cases of taco shells to be delivered to a "Lunch Lady."
That's me!
If you could just sign here.
Sure thing.
And here.
DWOOSH
Did you hear something?
I did.
I didn't hear anything

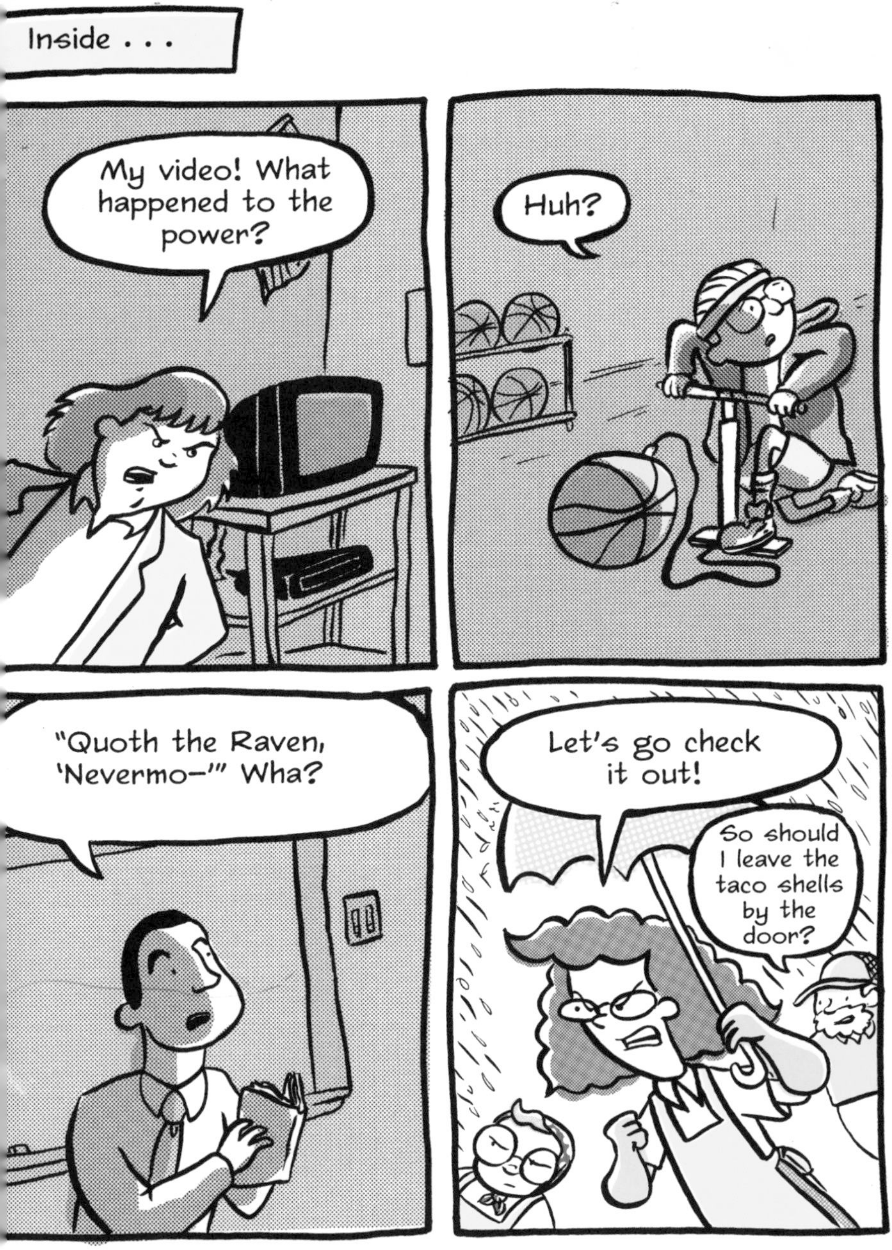
Inside . . .
My video! What happened to the power?
Huh?
"Quoth the Raven, 'Nevermo-'" Wha?
Let's go check it out!
So should I leave the taco shells by the door?

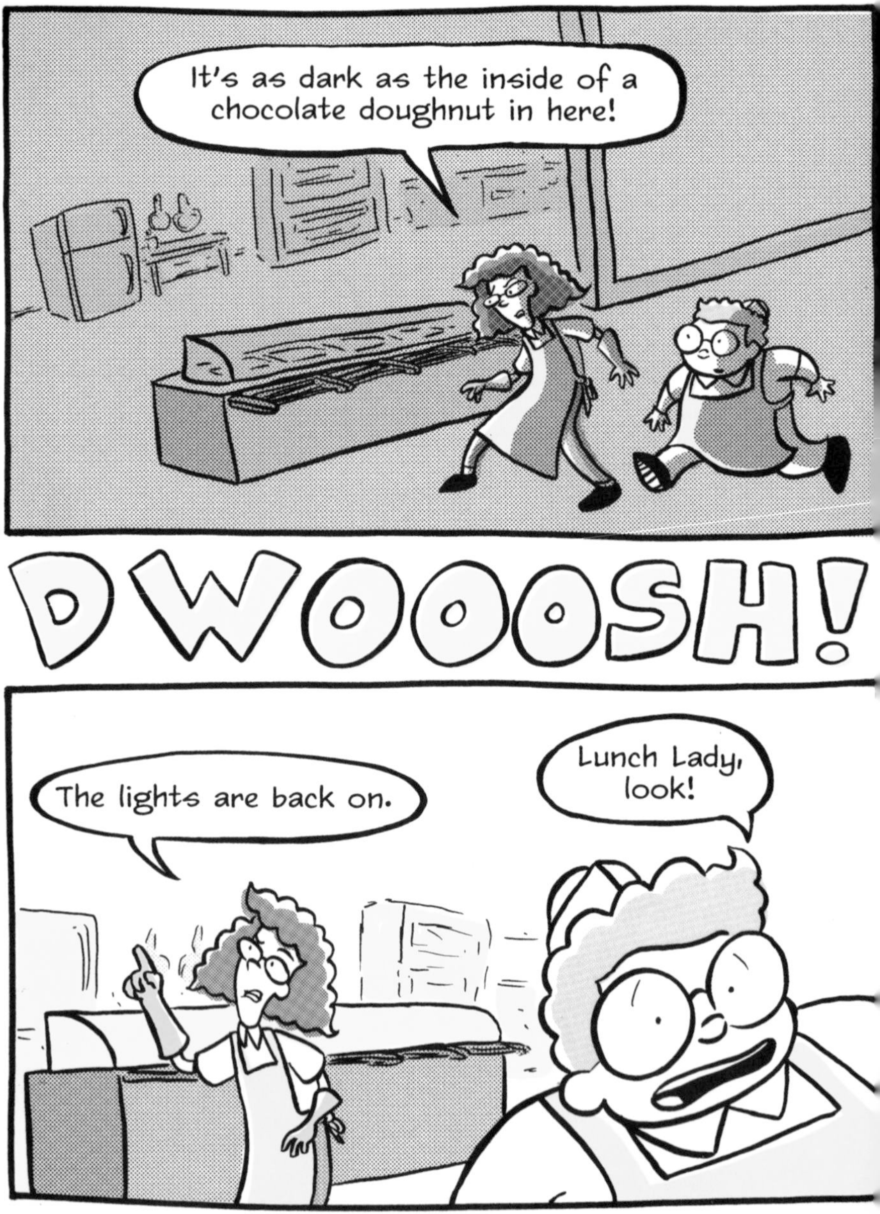
It's as dark as the inside of a chocolate doughnut in here!
DWOOOSH!
The lights are back on.
Lunch Lady, look!

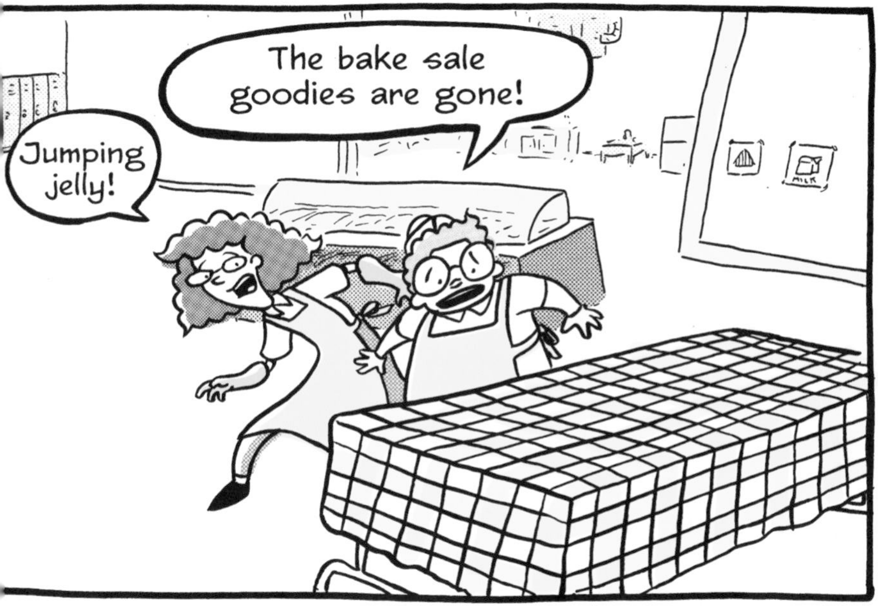
Jumping jelly!
The bake sale goodies are gone!

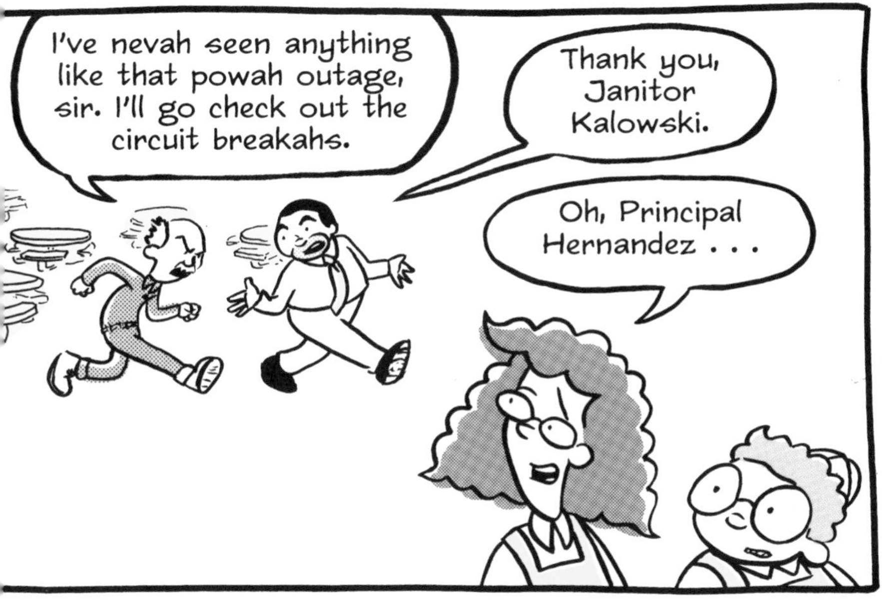
I've nevah seen anything like that powah outage, sir. I'll go check out the circuit breakahs.
Thank you, Janitor Kalowski.
Oh, Principal Hernandez . . .

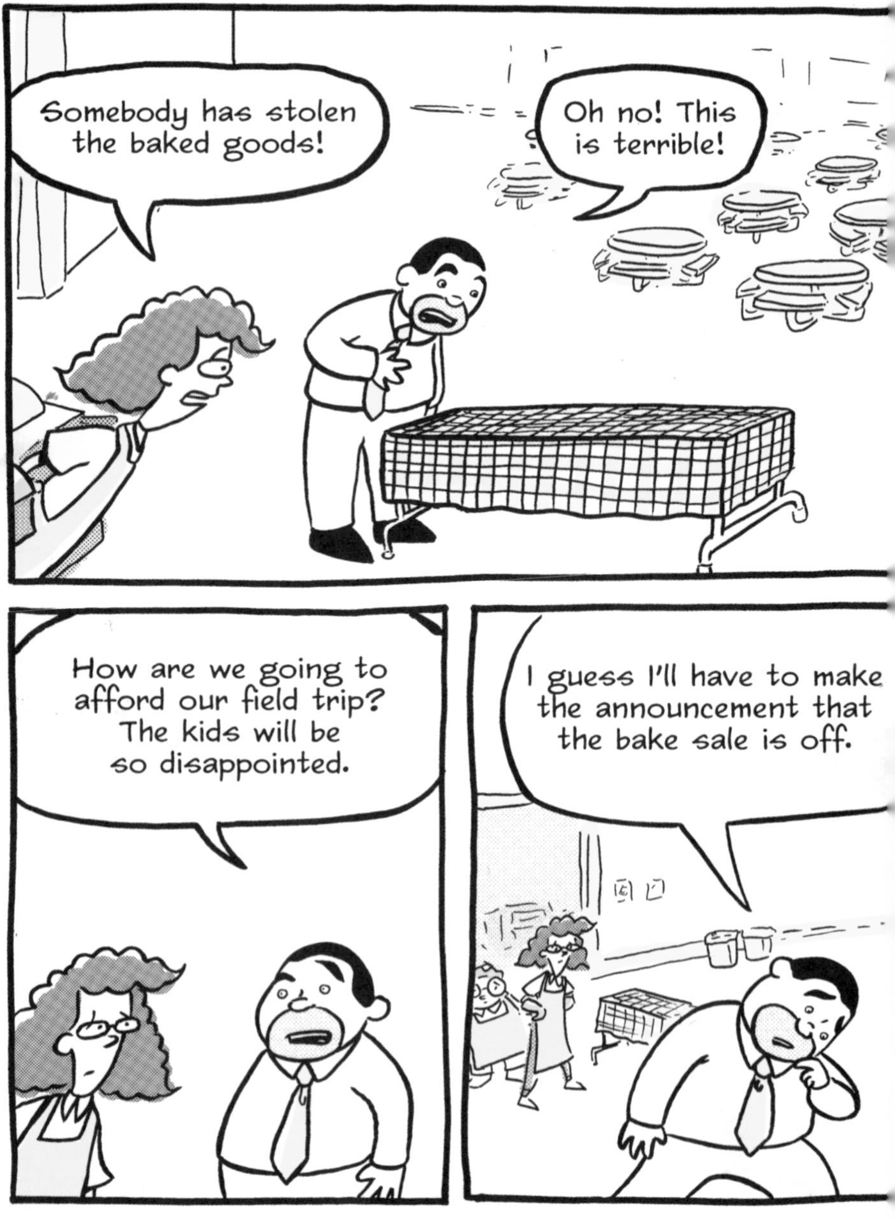
Somebody has stolen the baked goods!
Oh no! This is terrible!
How are we going to afford our field trip? The kids will be so disappointed.
I guess I'll have to make the announcement that the bake sale is off.

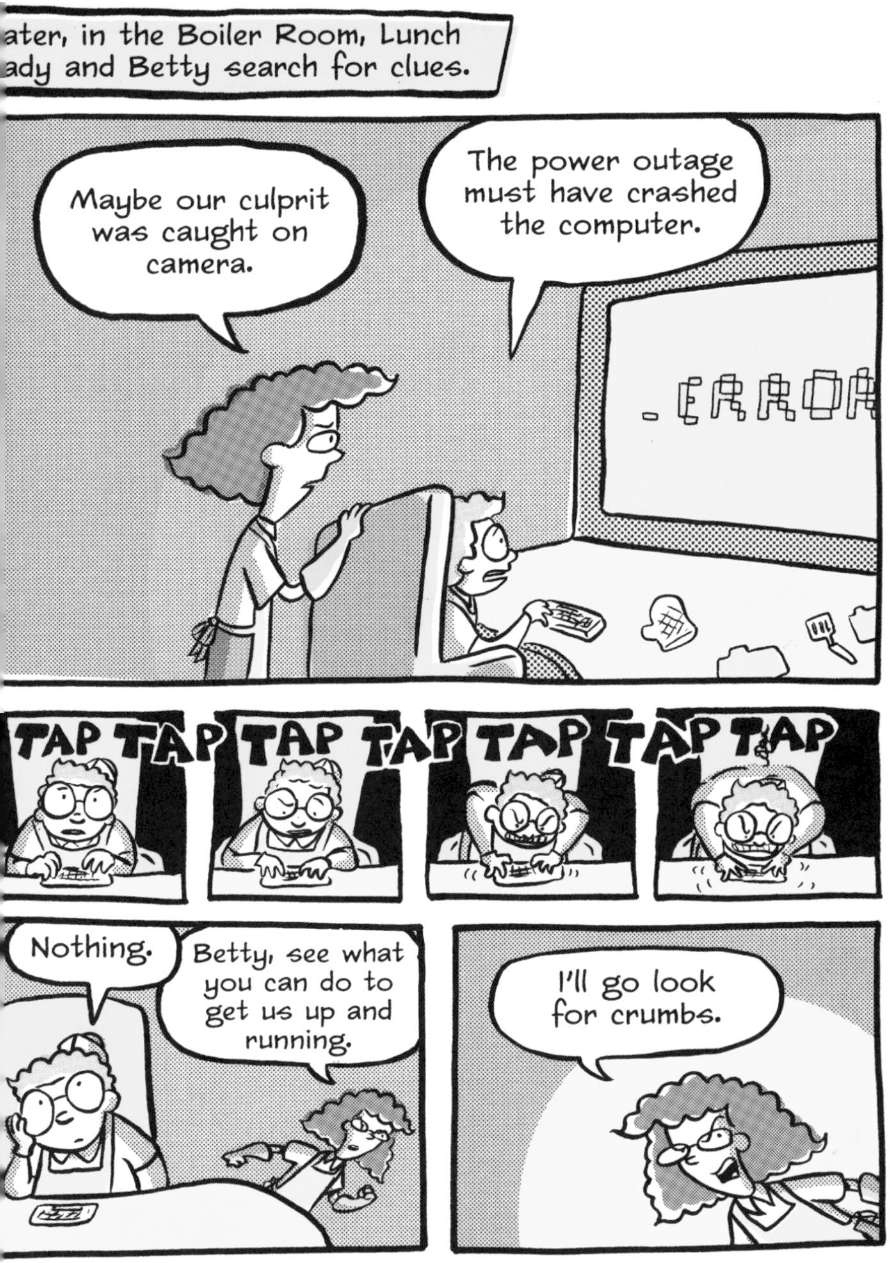

ater, in the Boiler Room, Lunch
ady and Betty search for clues.
Maybe our culprit was caught on camera.
The power outage must have crashed the computer.
ERROR
TAP TAP TAP TAP TAP TAP TAP
Nothing.
Betty, see what you can do to get us up and running.
I'll go look for crumbs.

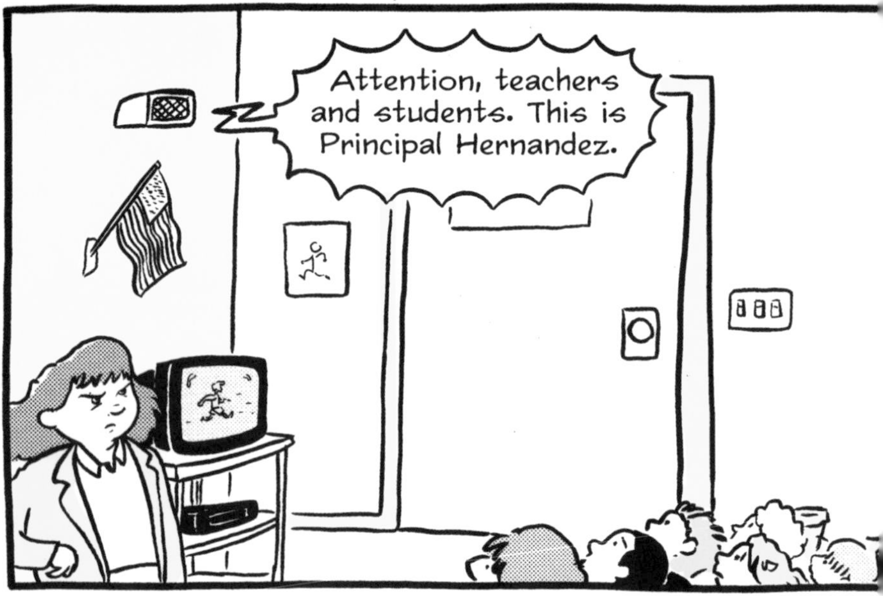
Attention, teachers and students. This is Principal Hernandez.

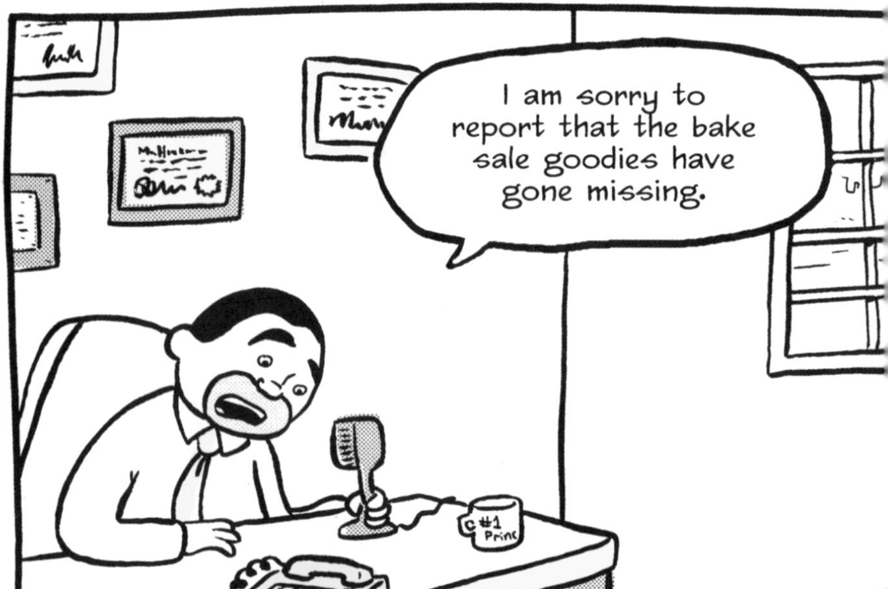
I am sorry to report that the bake sale goodies have gone missing.
#1 Princ

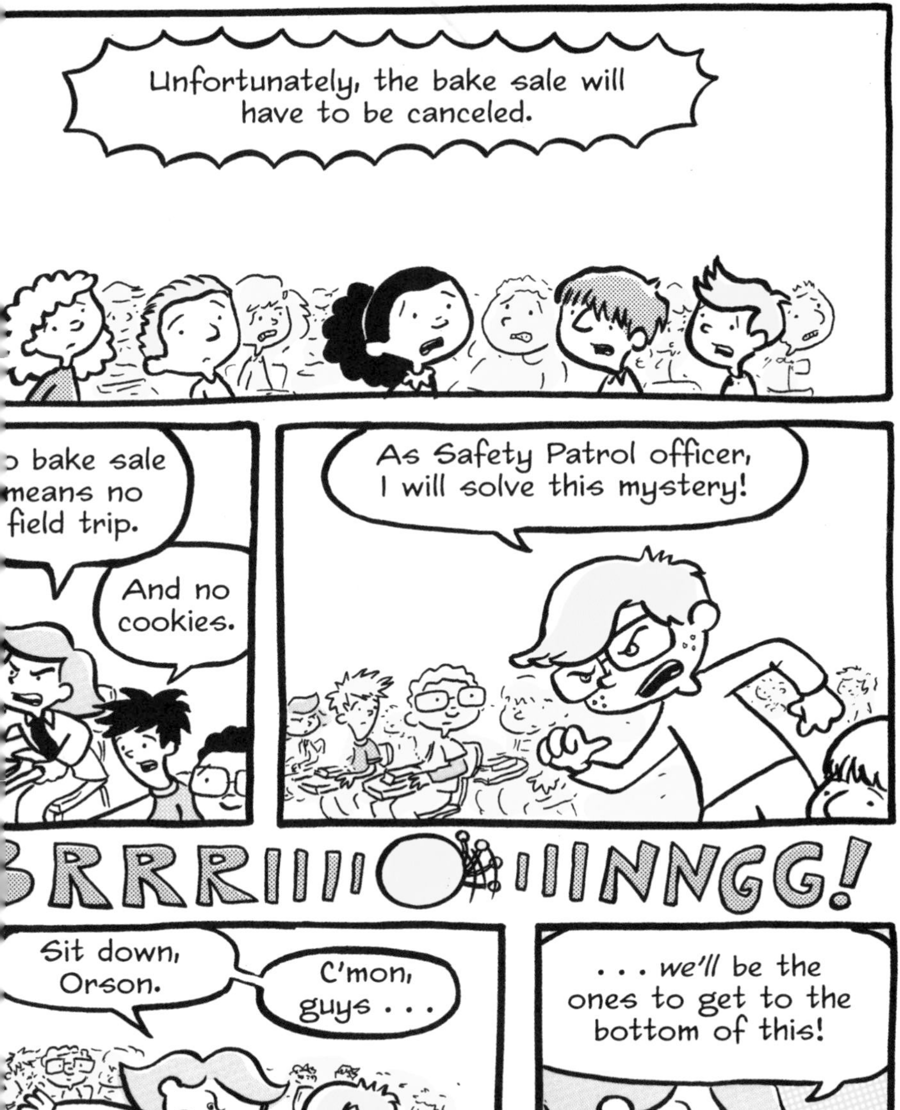
Unfortunately, the bake sale will have to be canceled.
o bake sale means no field trip.
And no cookies.
As Safety Patrol officer, I will solve this mystery!
RRRIIIIIIINNGG!
Sit down, Orson.
C'mon, guys . . .
. . . *we'll* be the ones to get to the bottom of this!

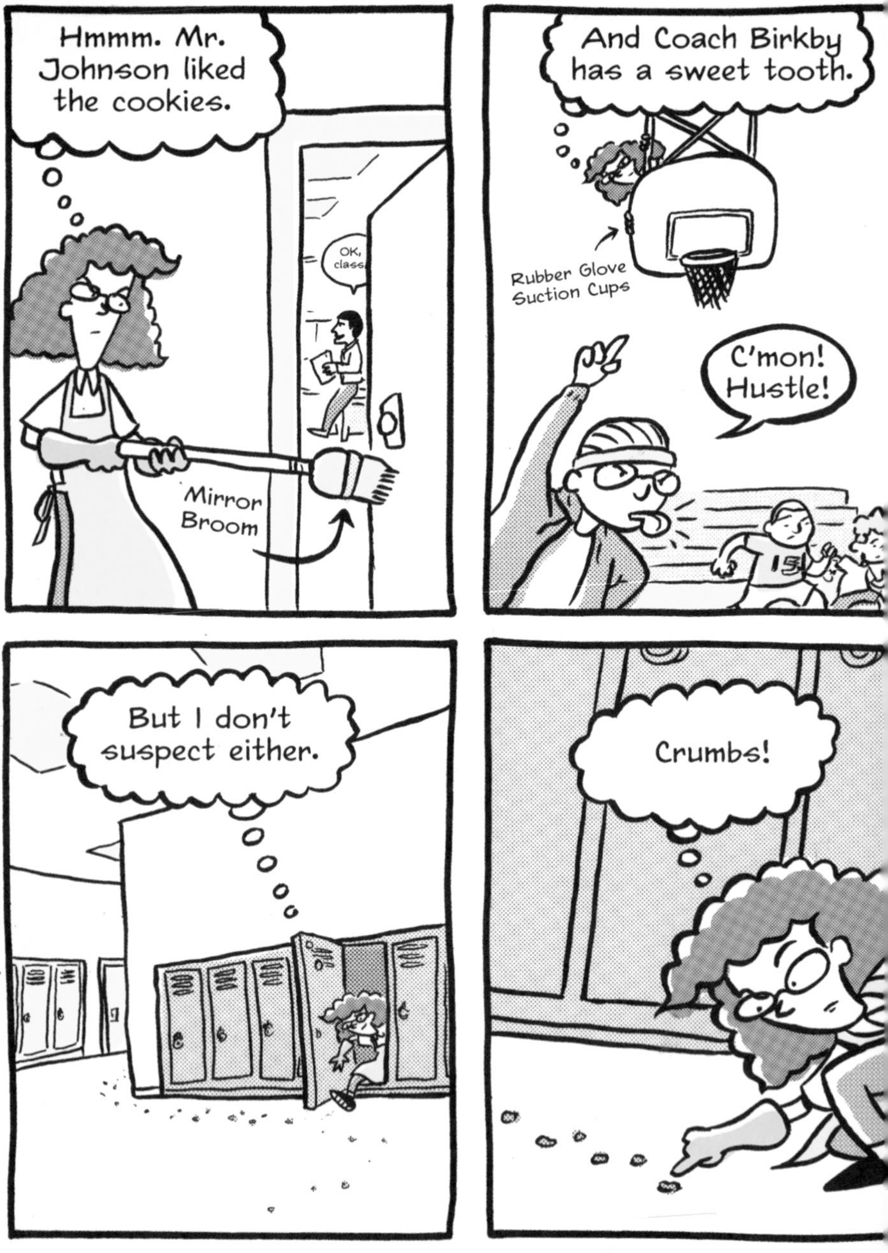
Hmmm. Mr. Johnson liked the cookies.
OK, class
Mirror Broom
And Coach Birkby has a sweet tooth.
Rubber Glove Suction Cups
C'mon! Hustle!
But I don't suspect either.
Crumbs!

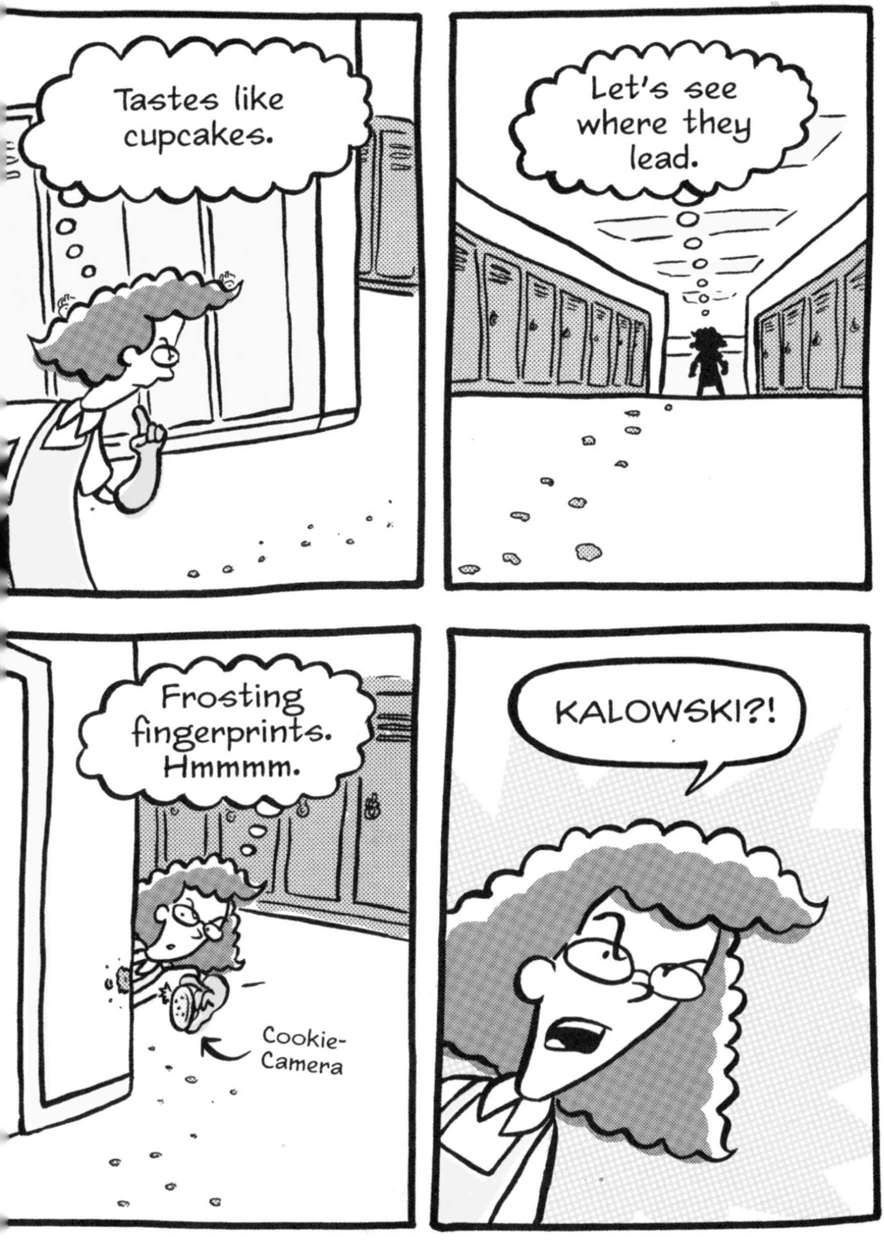
Tastes like cupcakes.
Let's see where they lead.
Frosting fingerprints. Hmmmm.
Cookie-Camera
KALOWSKI?!

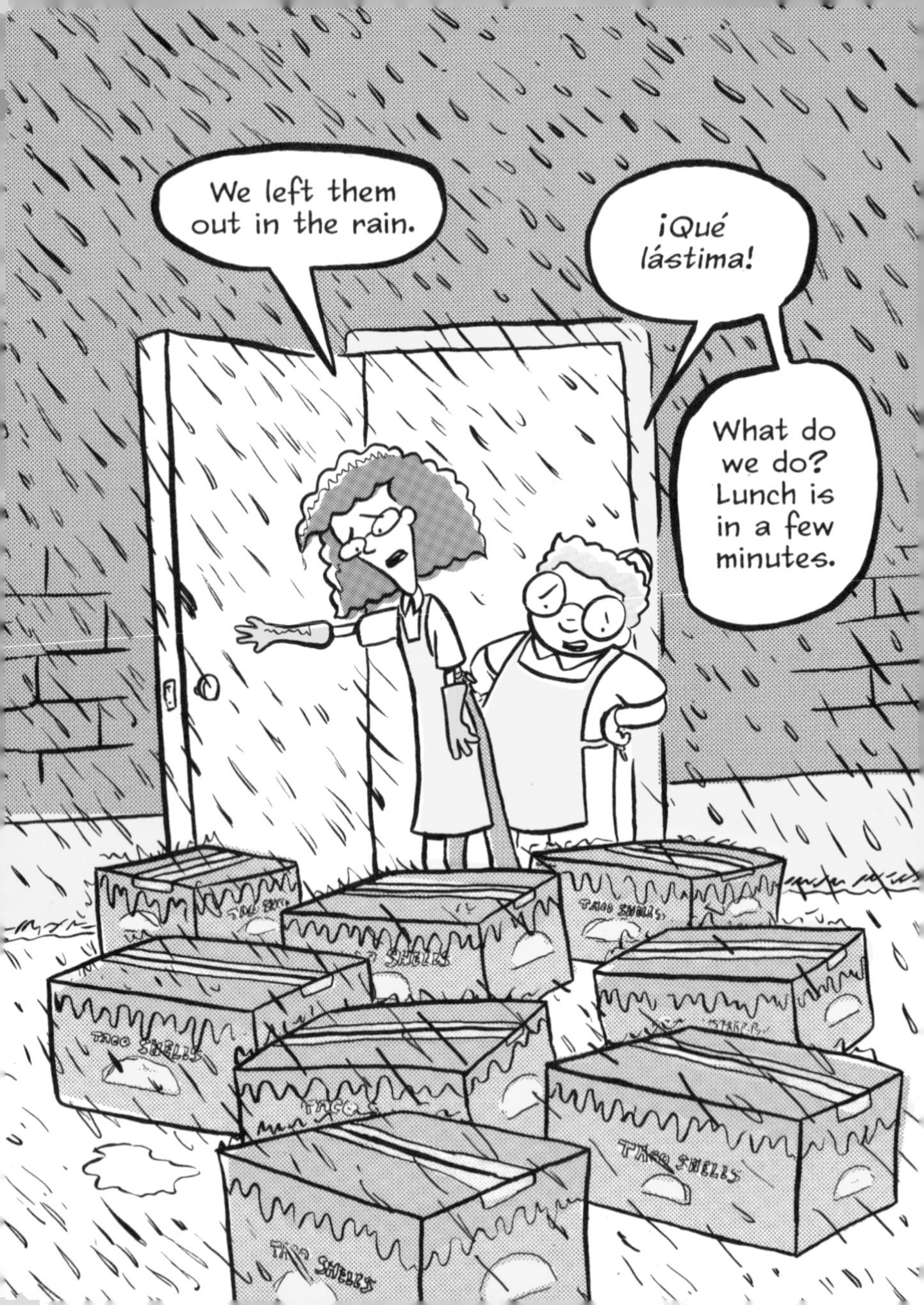
We left them out in the rain.
¡Qué lástima!
What do we do? Lunch is in a few minutes.
TACO SHELLS

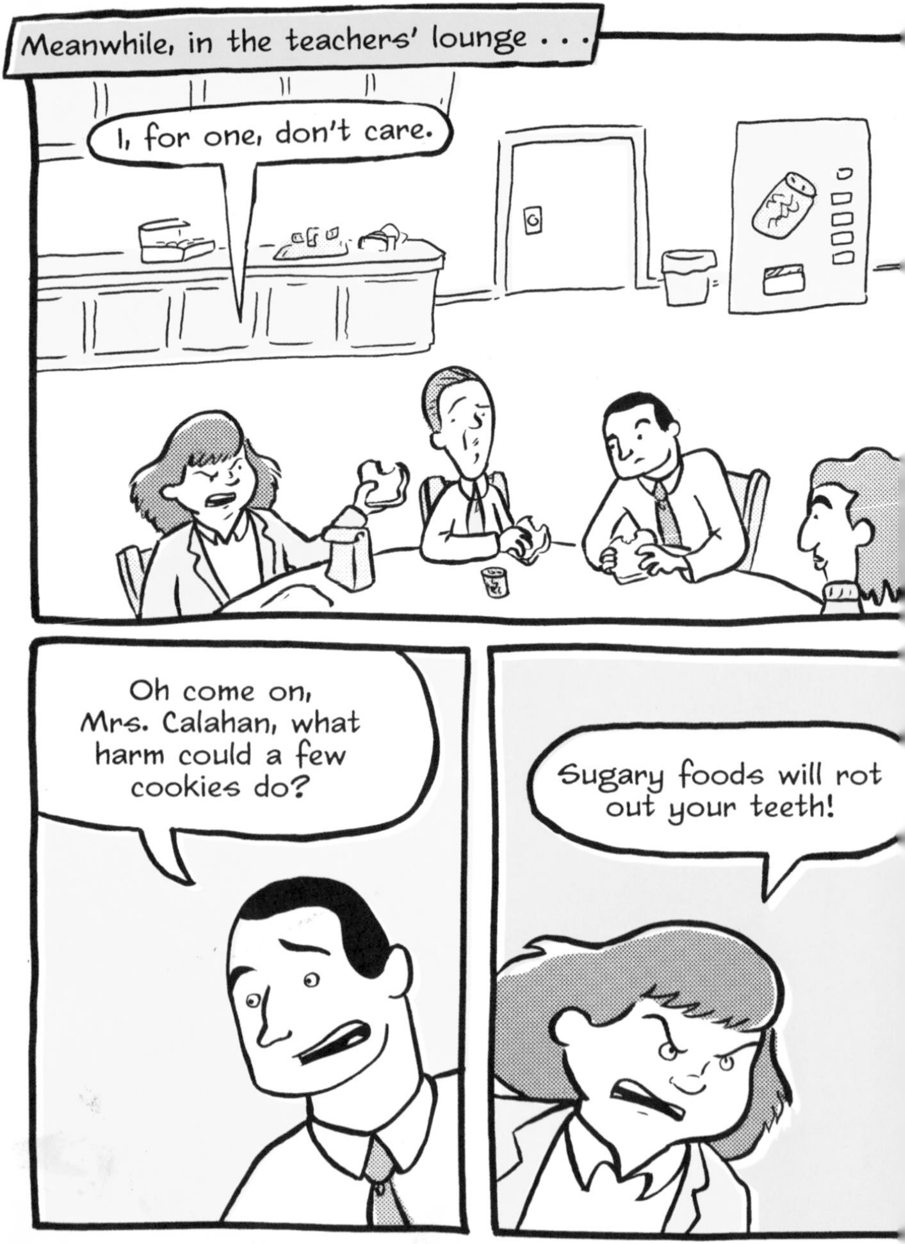
Meanwhile, in the teachers' lounge . . .
I, for one, don't care.
Oh come on, Mrs. Calahan, what harm could a few cookies do?
Sugary foods will rot out your teeth!

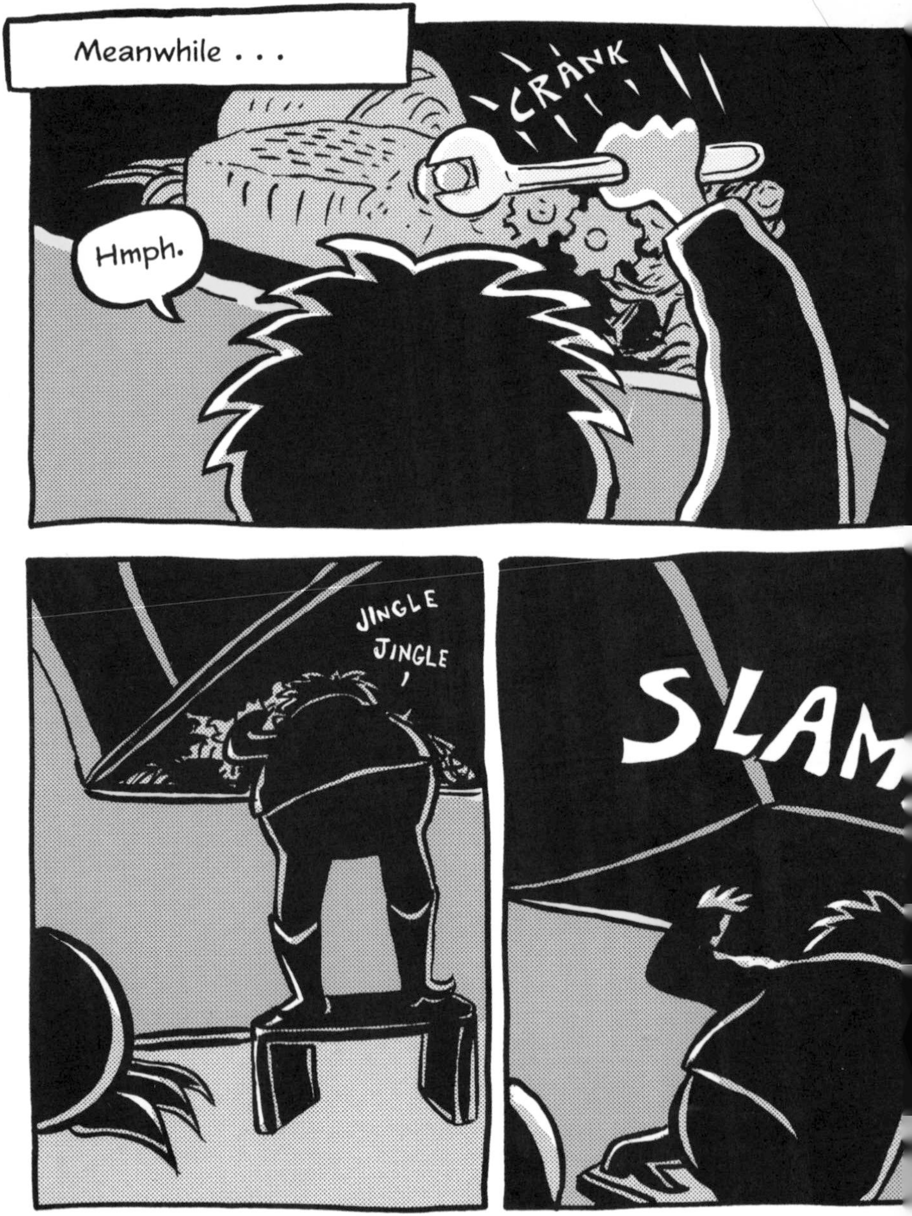
Meanwhile . . .
CRANK
Hmph.
JINGLE
JINGLE
SLAM

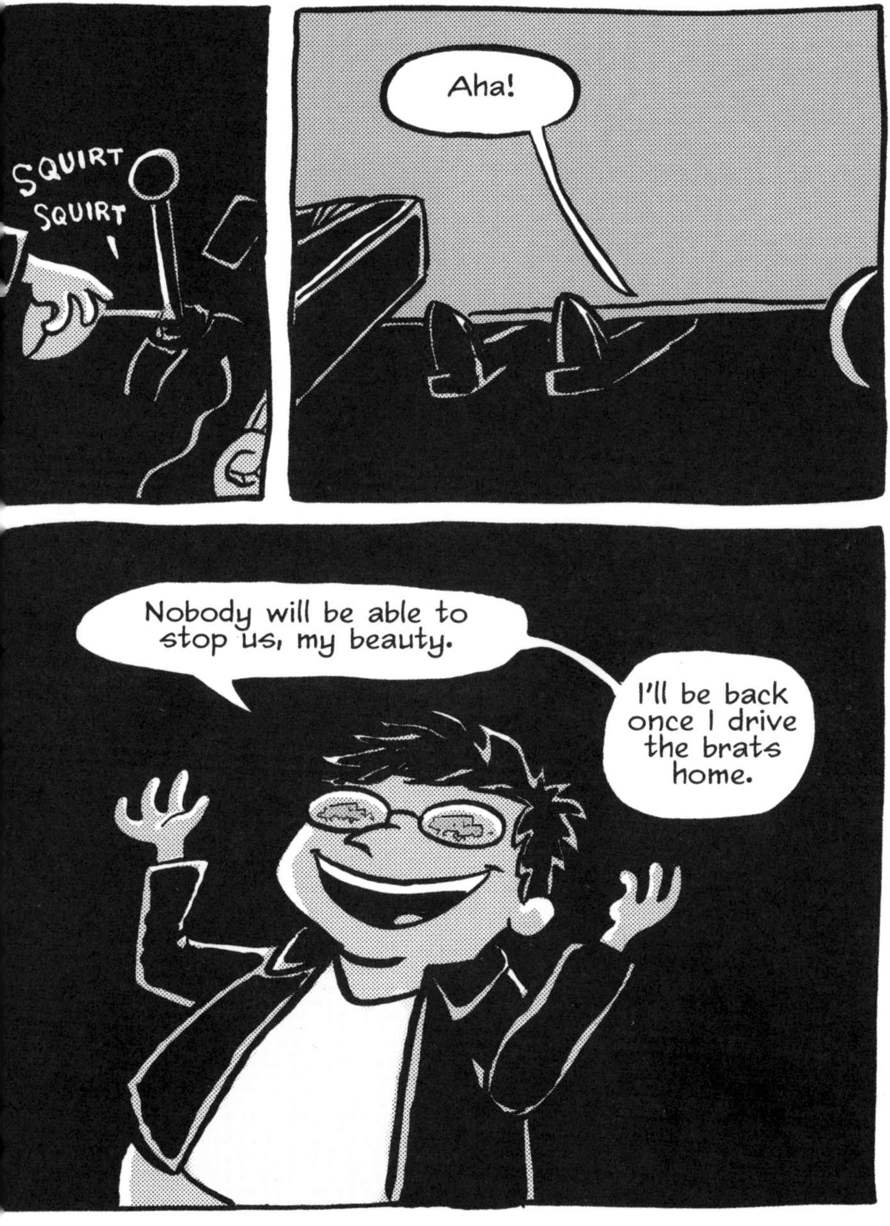
SQUIRT
SQUIRT
Aha!
Nobody will be able to stop us, my beauty.
I'll be back once I drive the brats home.

BRRRıııı◯ıııINNGG

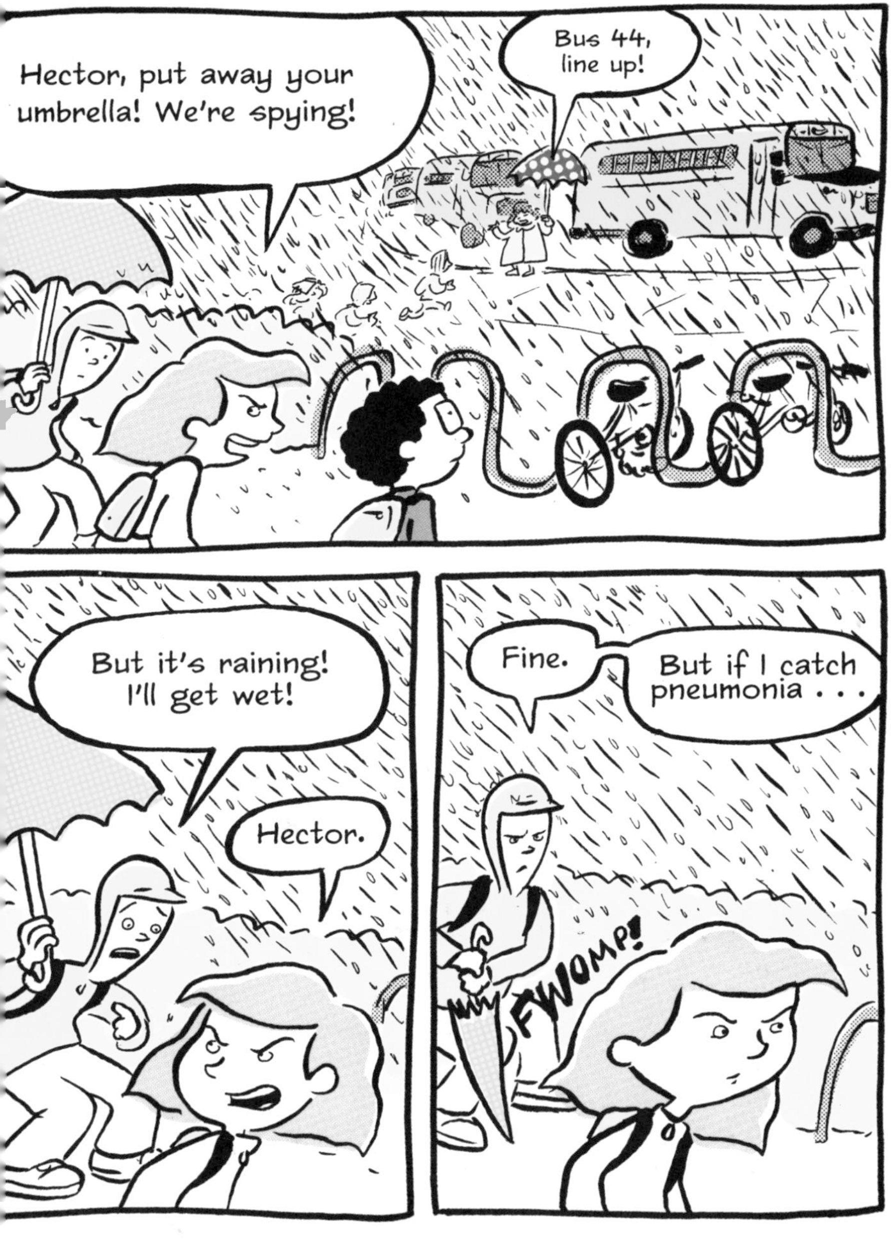
Hector, put away your umbrella! We're spying!
Bus 44, line up!
But it's raining! I'll get wet!
Hector.
Fine.
But if I catch pneumonia . . .
FWOMP!

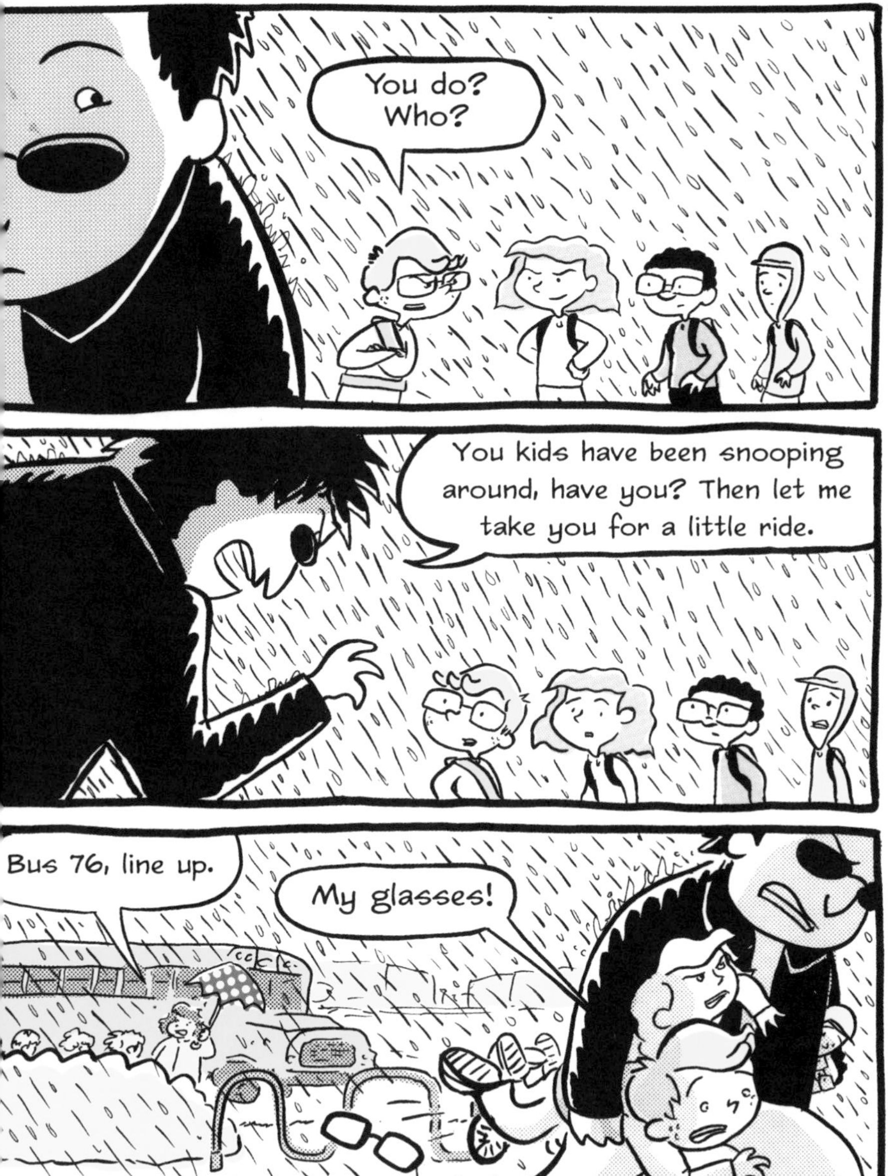
You do? Who?
You kids have been snooping around, have you? Then let me take you for a little ride.
Bus 76, line up.
My glasses!

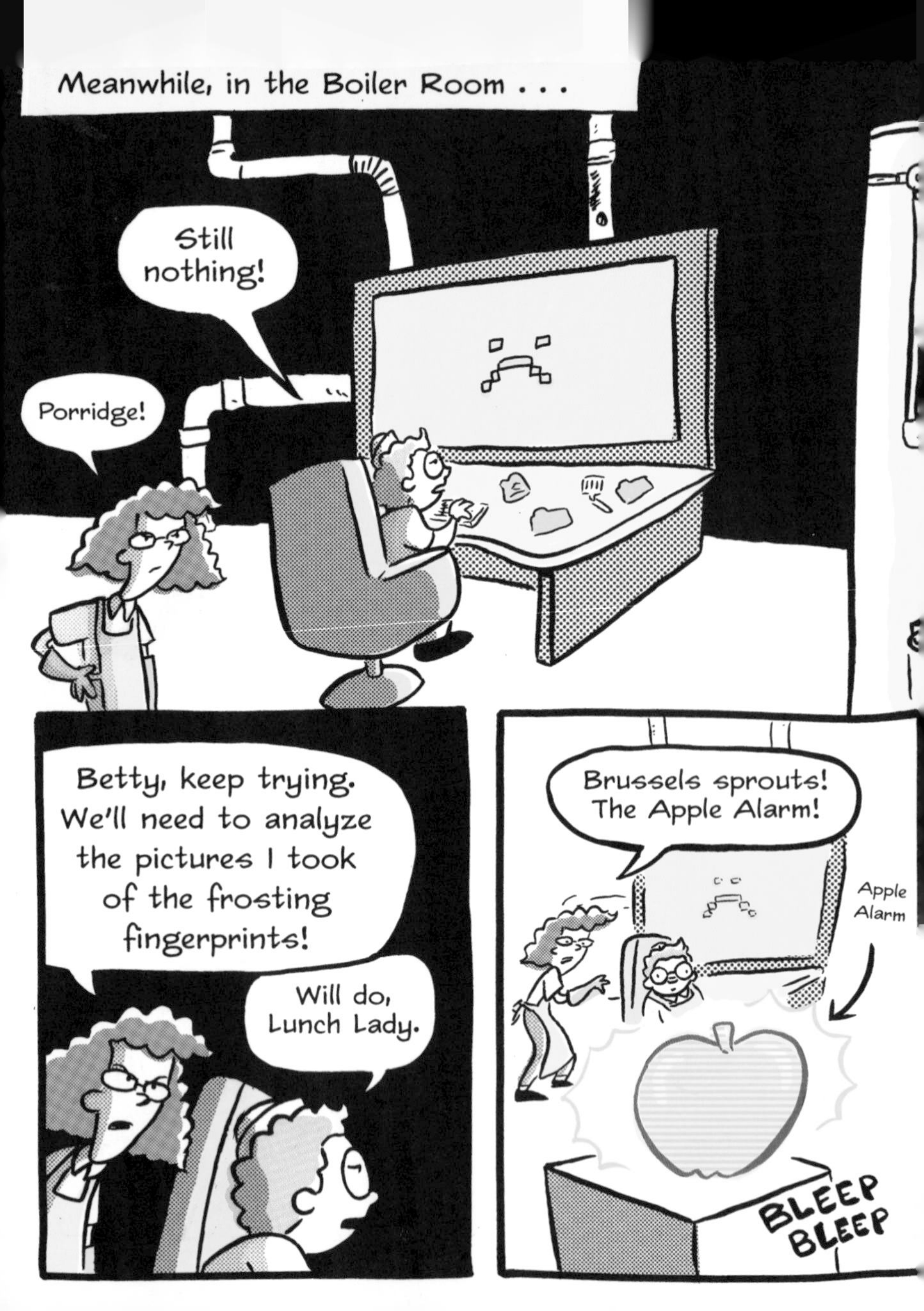
Meanwhile, in the Boiler Room . . .
Still nothing!
Porridge!
Betty, keep trying. We'll need to analyze the pictures I took of the frosting fingerprints!
Will do, Lunch Lady.
Brussels sprouts! The Apple Alarm!
Apple Alarm
BLEEP BLEEP

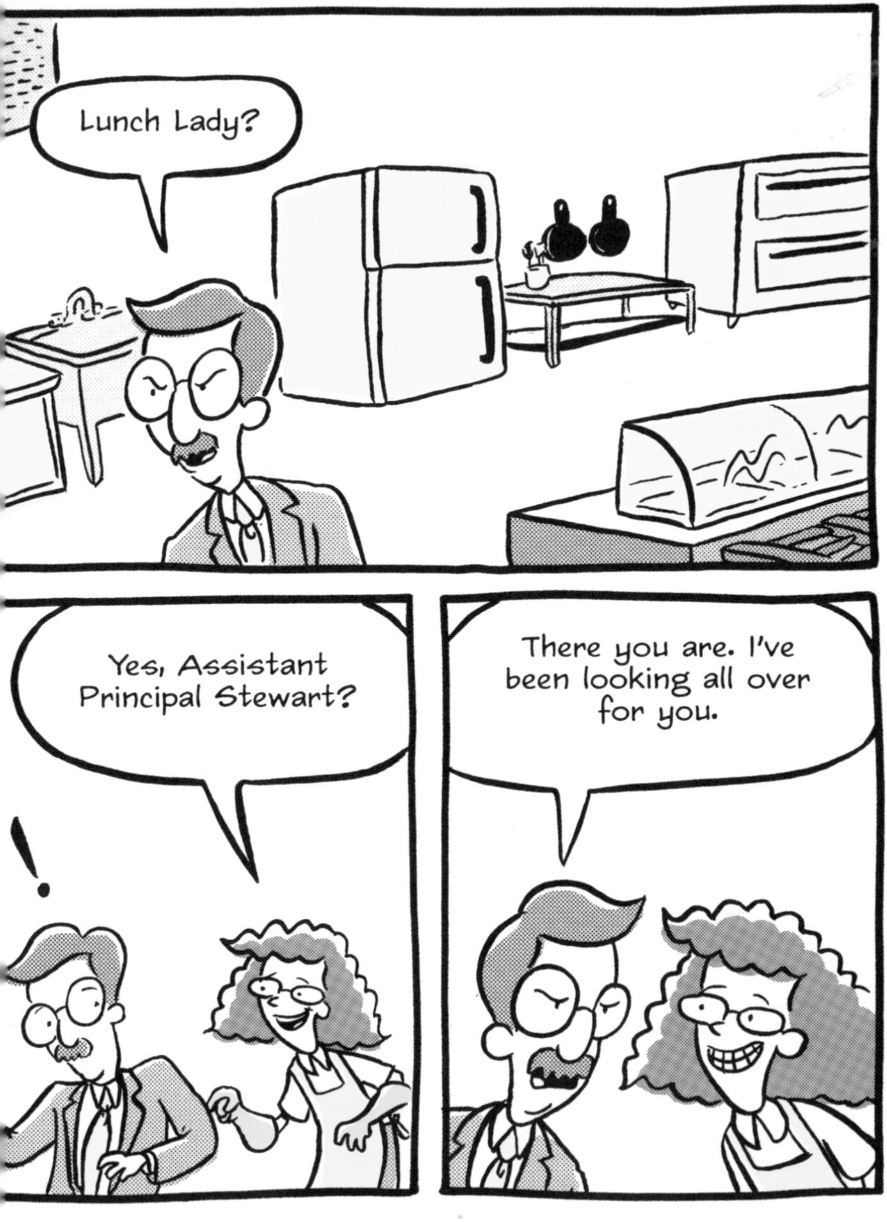
Lunch Lady?
Yes, Assistant Principal Stewart?
There you are. I've been looking all over for you.

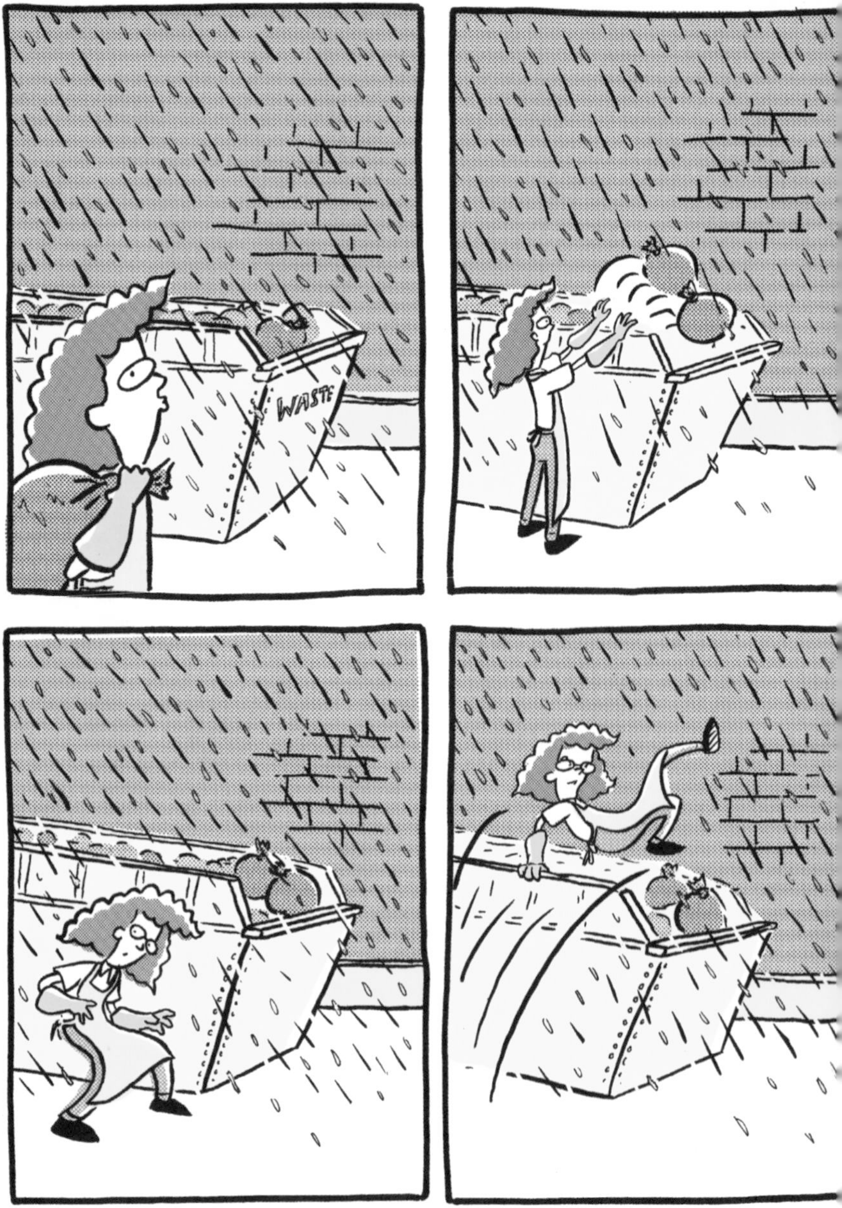
WASTE

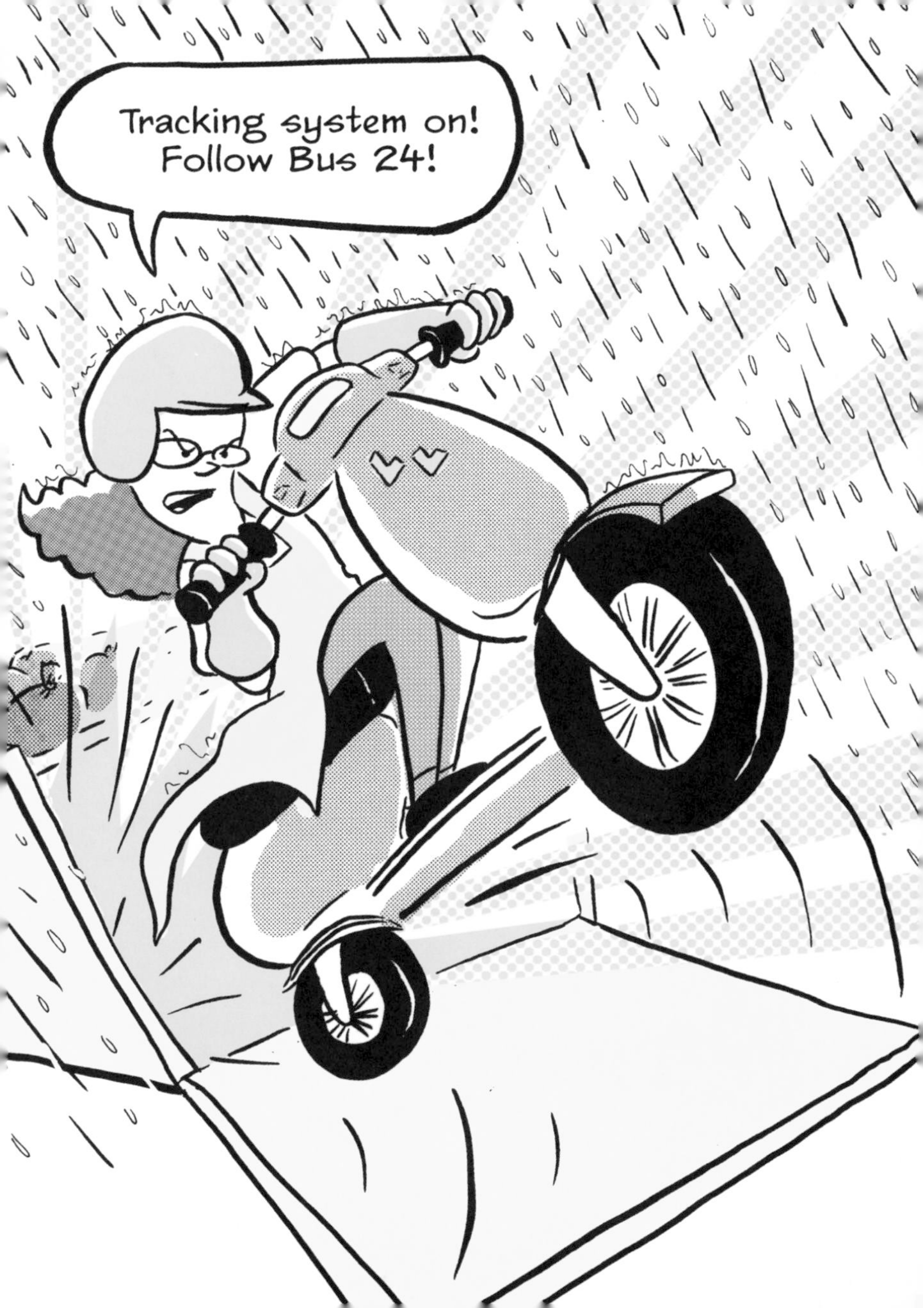
Tracking system on!
Follow Bus 24!

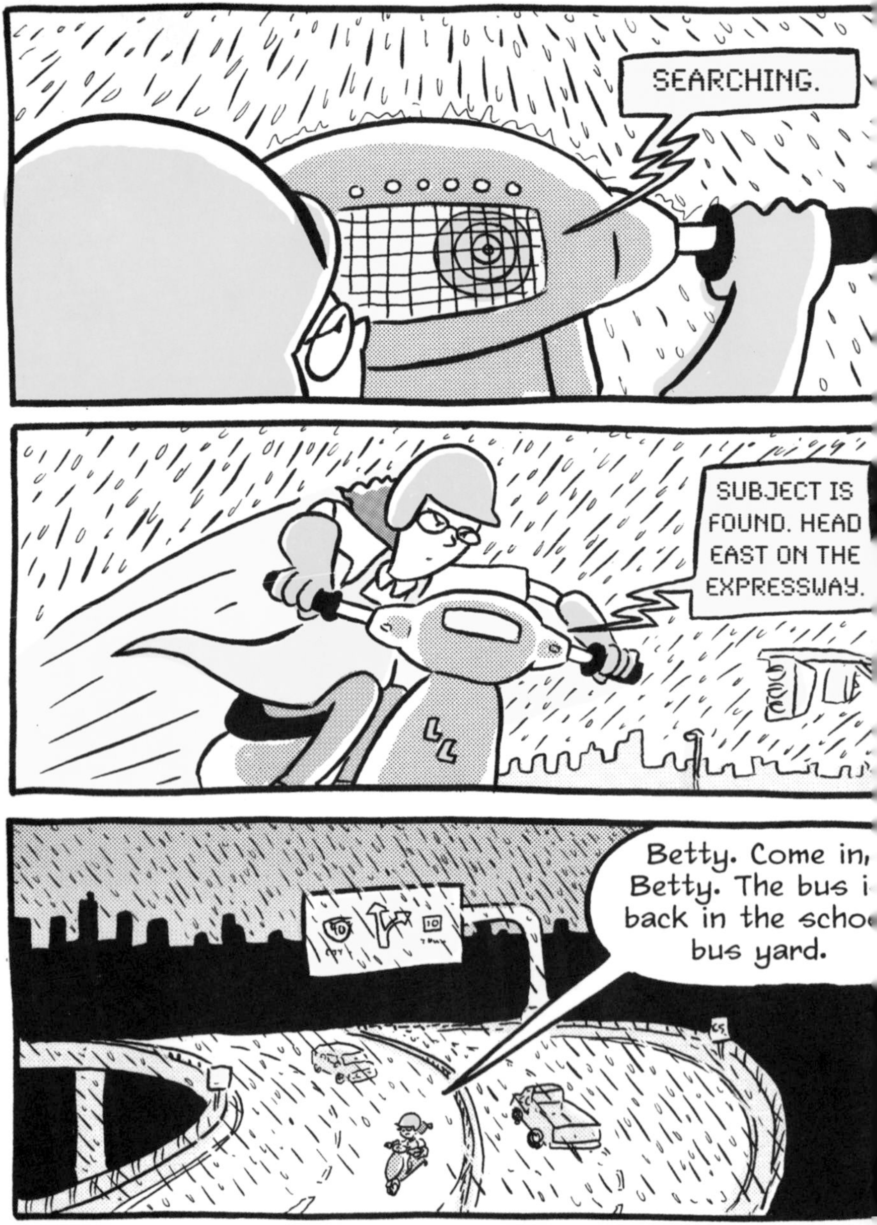
SEARCHING.
SUBJECT IS FOUND. HEAD EAST ON THE EXPRESSWAY.
Betty. Come in, Betty. The bus i back in the scho bus yard.

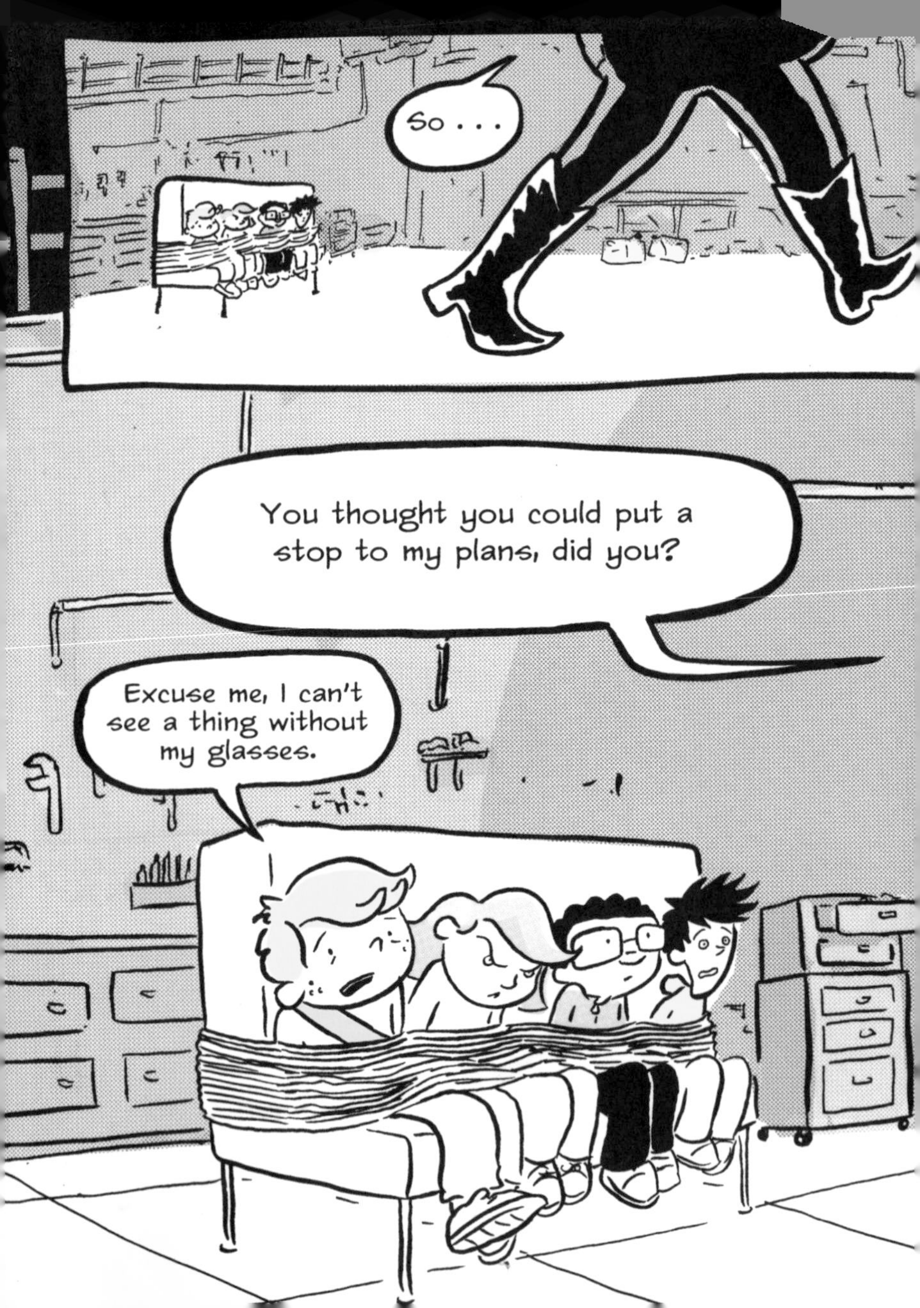
So . . .
You thought you could put a stop to my plans, did you?
Excuse me, I can't see a thing without my glasses.

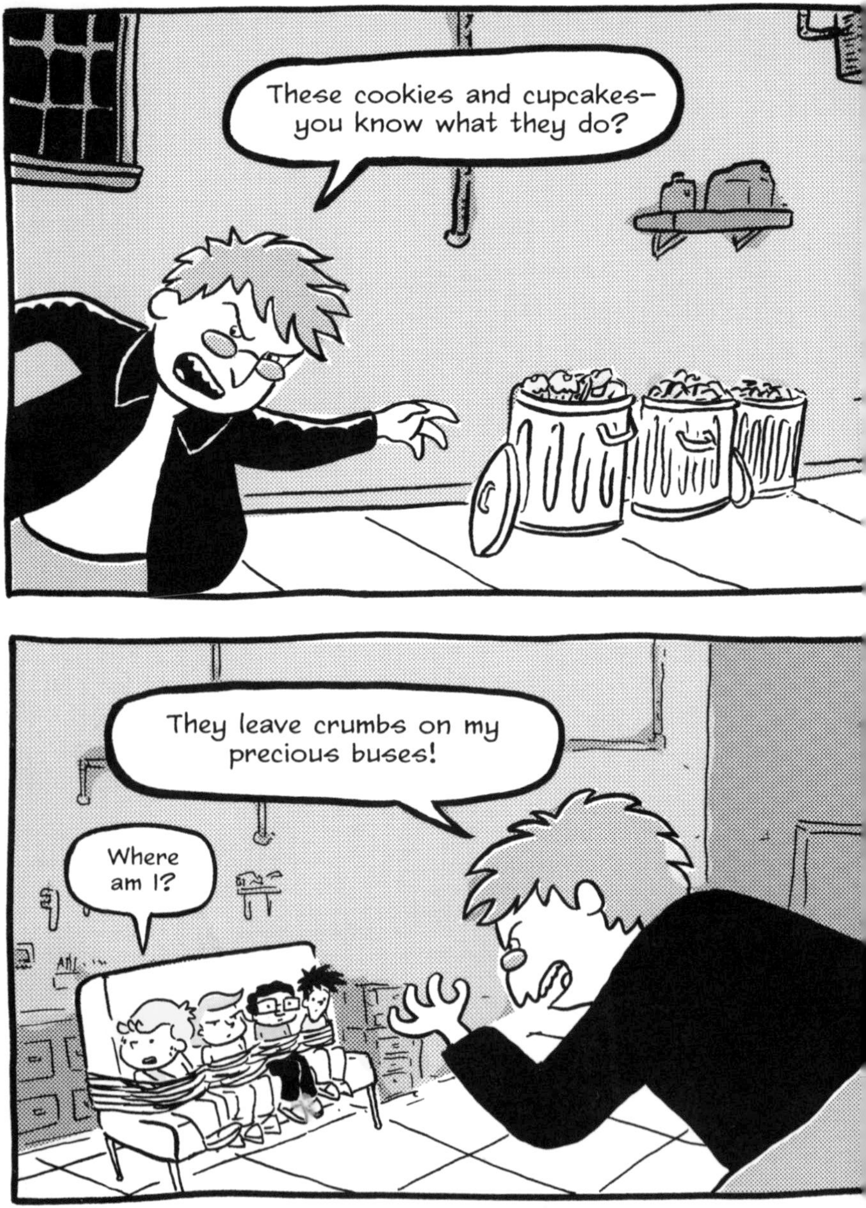
These cookies and cupcakes-
you know what they do?
They leave crumbs on my
precious buses!
Where
am I?

Betty, I'm atop the garage in the school bus yard!
Now to find bus driver Brenda.
I'm on my way!

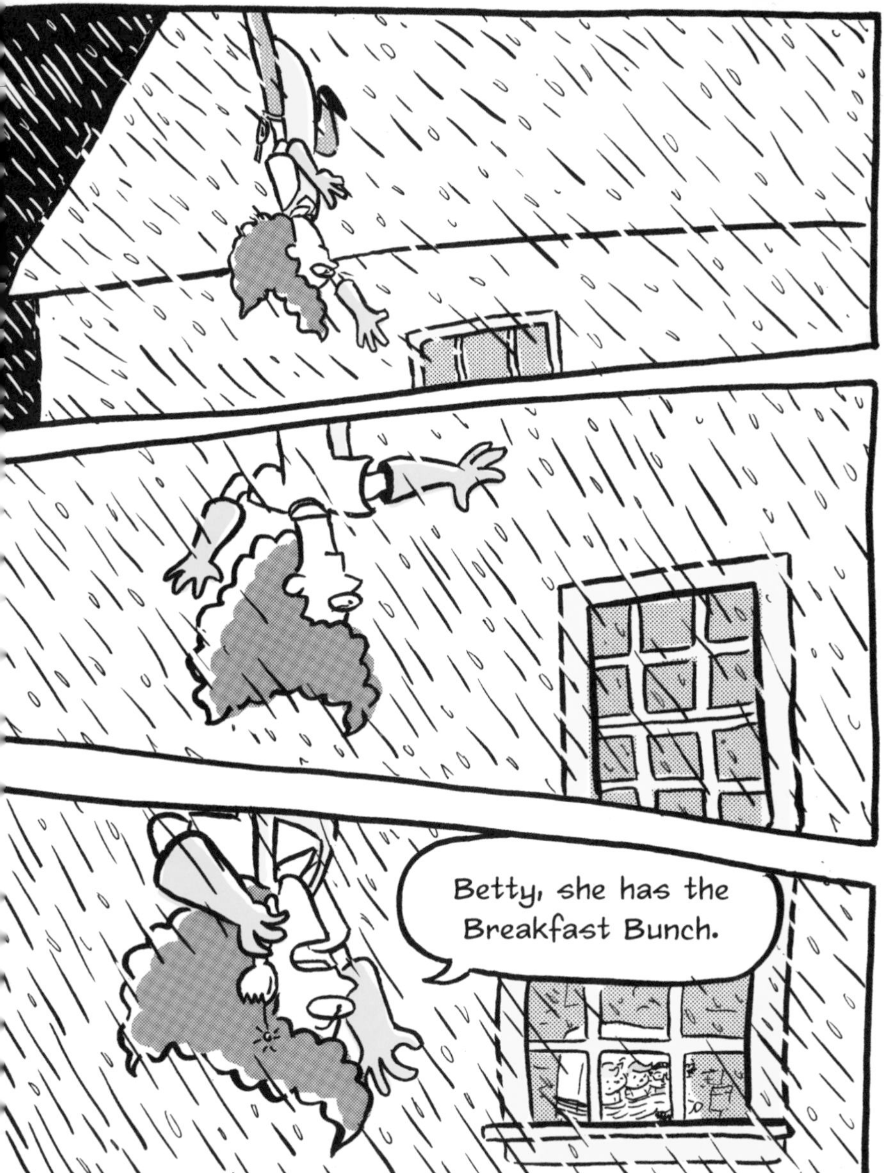
Betty, she has the Breakfast Bunch.

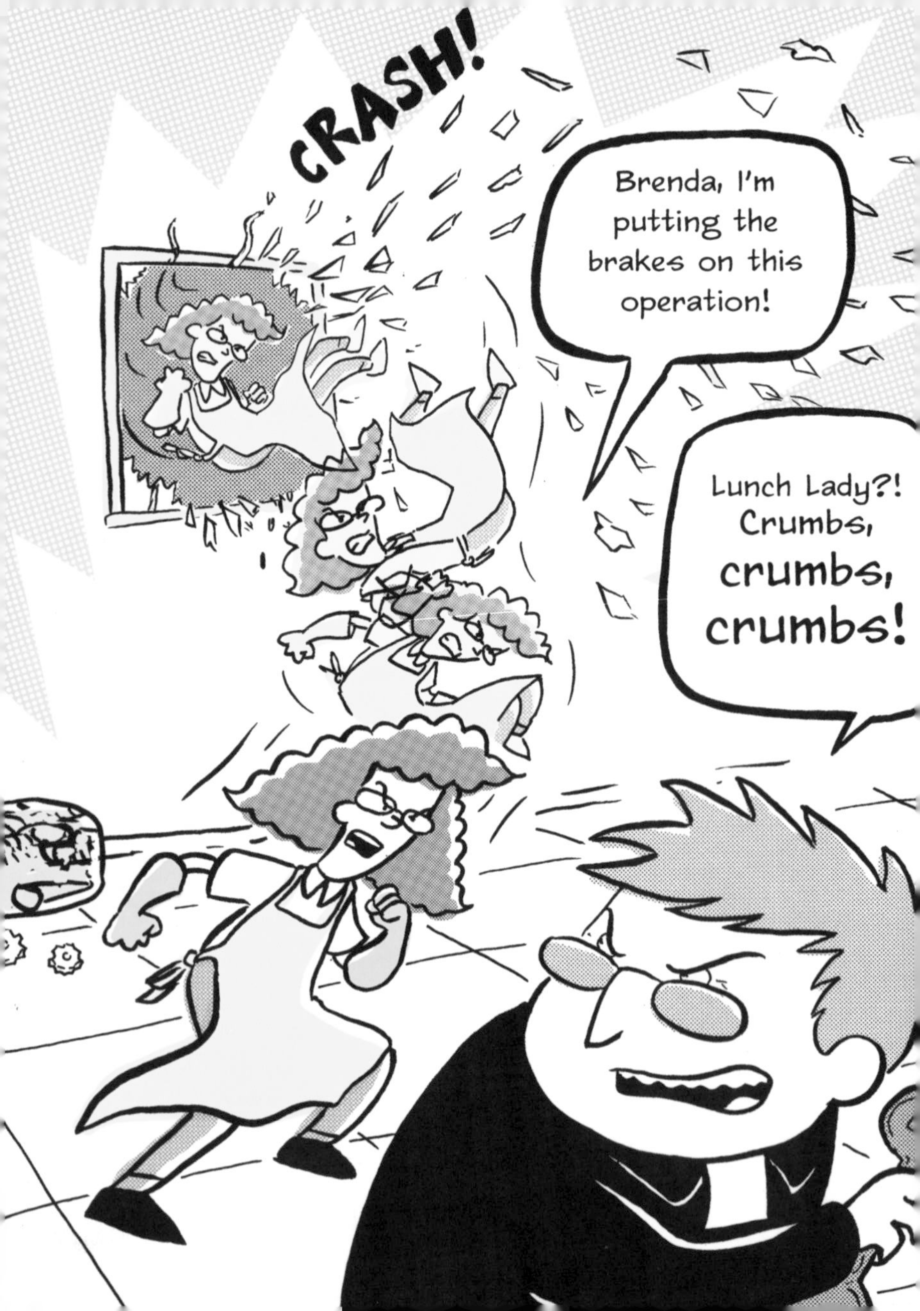
CRASH!
Brenda, I'm putting the brakes on this operation!
Lunch Lady?! Crumbs, crumbs, crumbs!

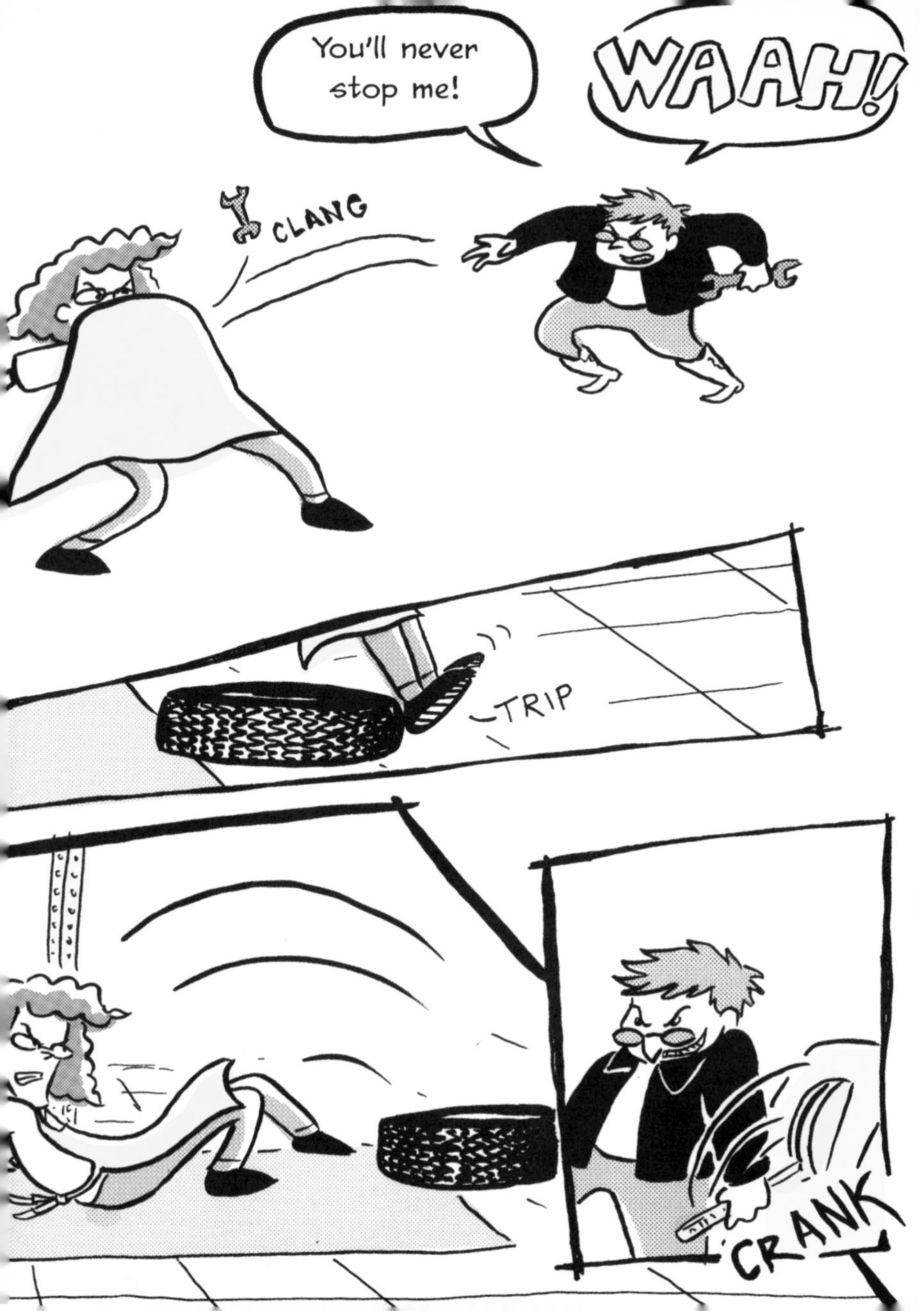
You'll never stop me!
WAAH!
CLANG
TRIP
CRANK

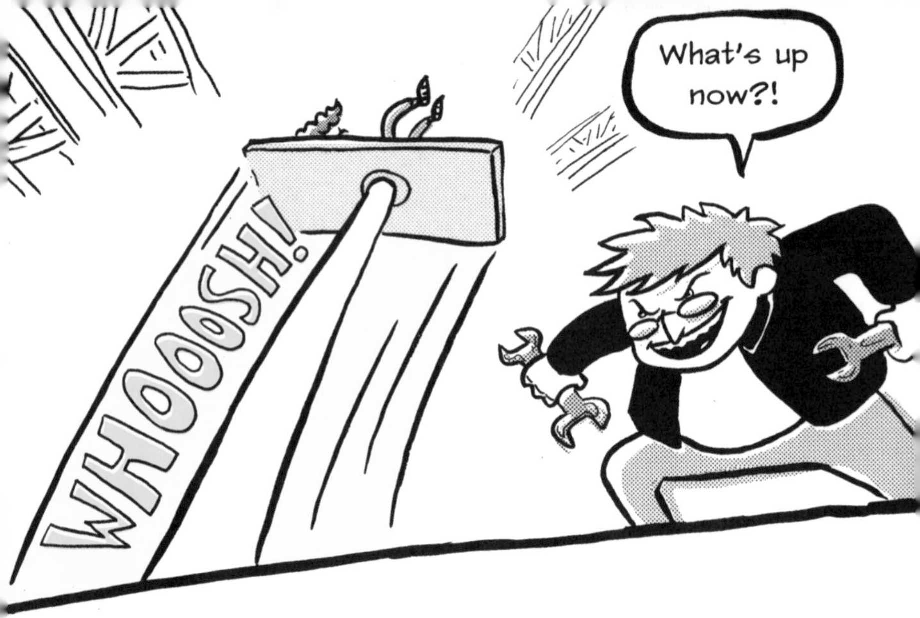
WHOOOSH!
What's up now?!

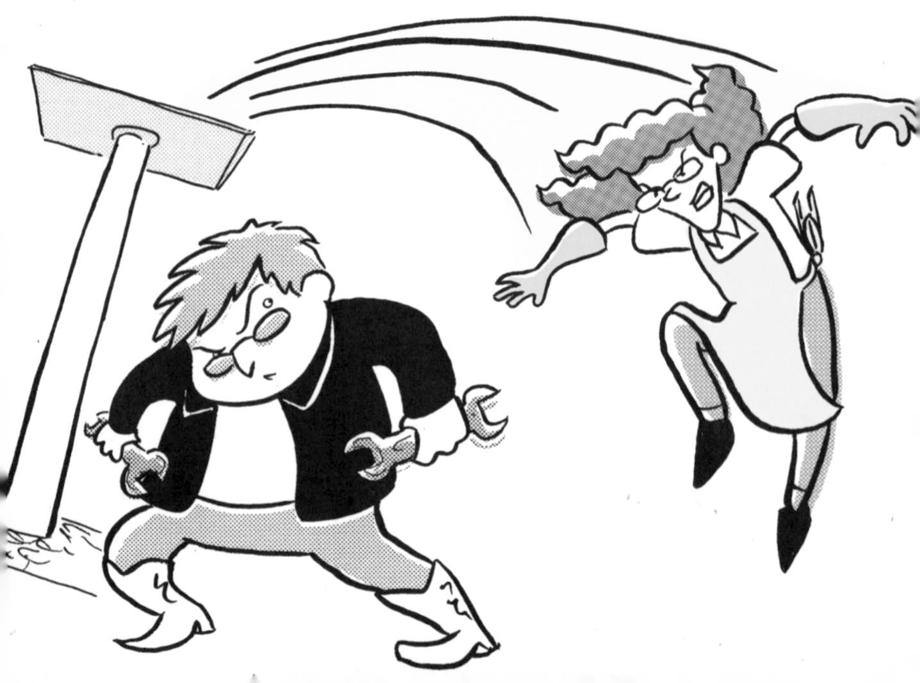

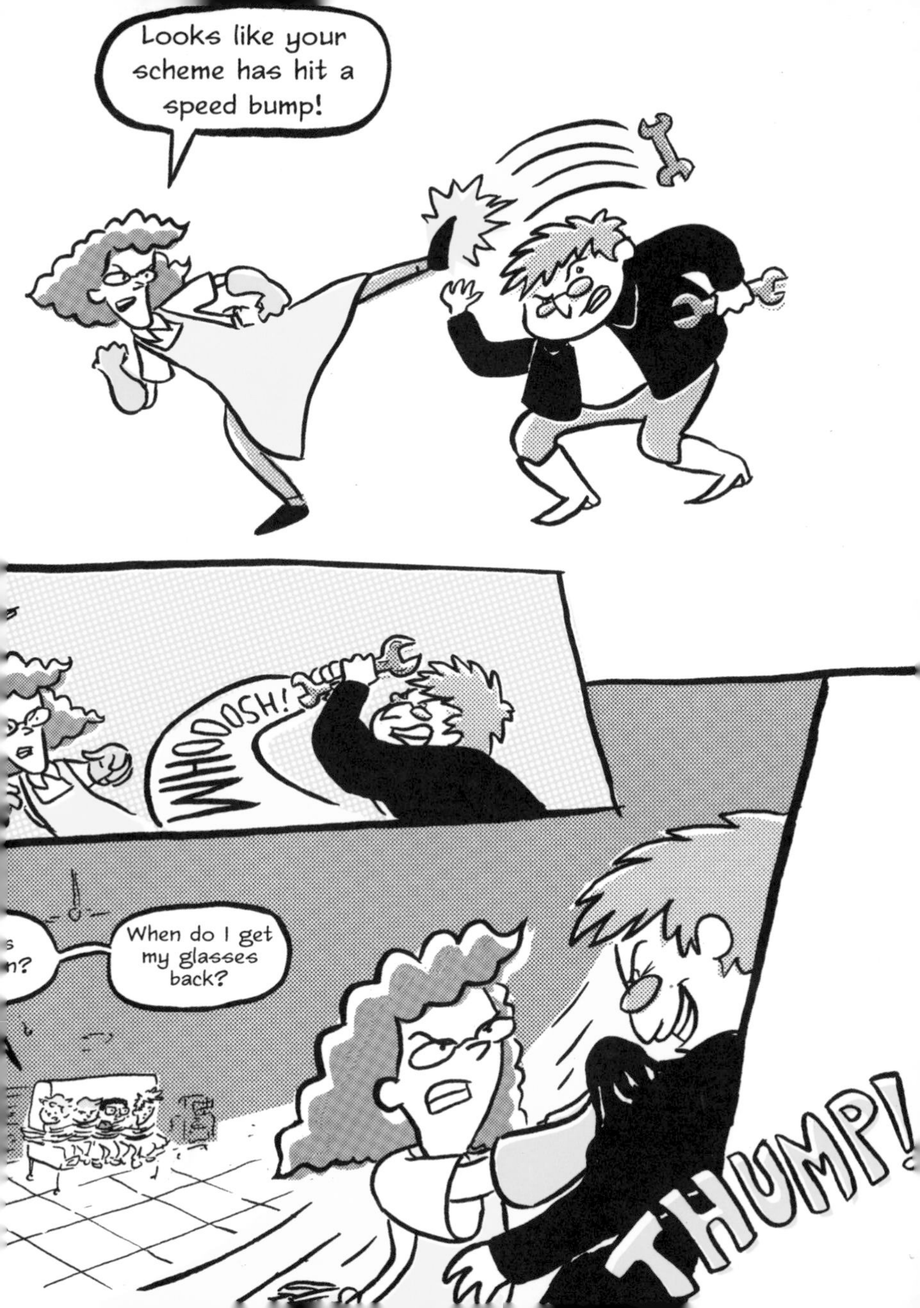
Looks like your scheme has hit a speed bump!
WHOOOSH!
When do I get my glasses back?
THUMP!

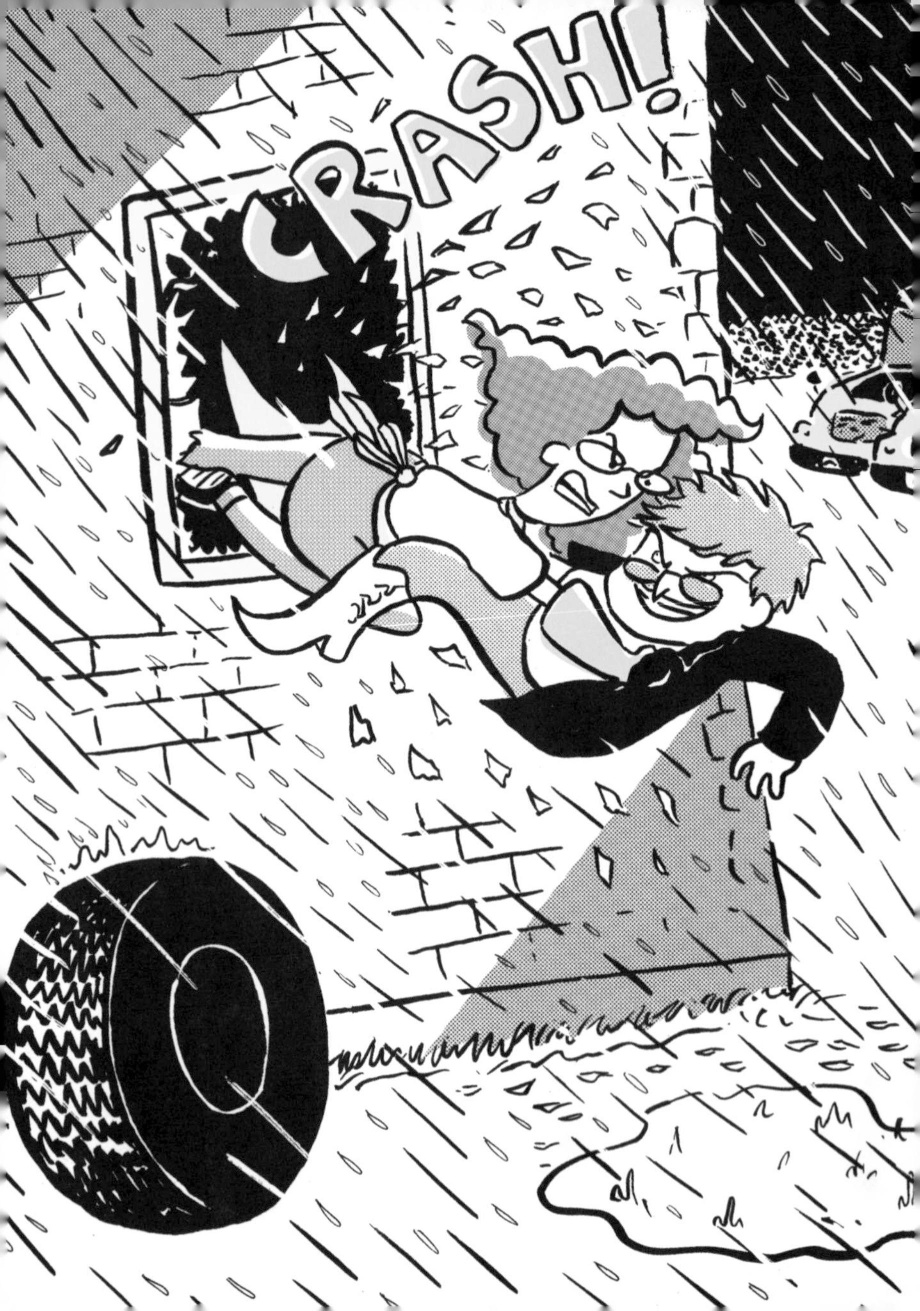
CRASH!

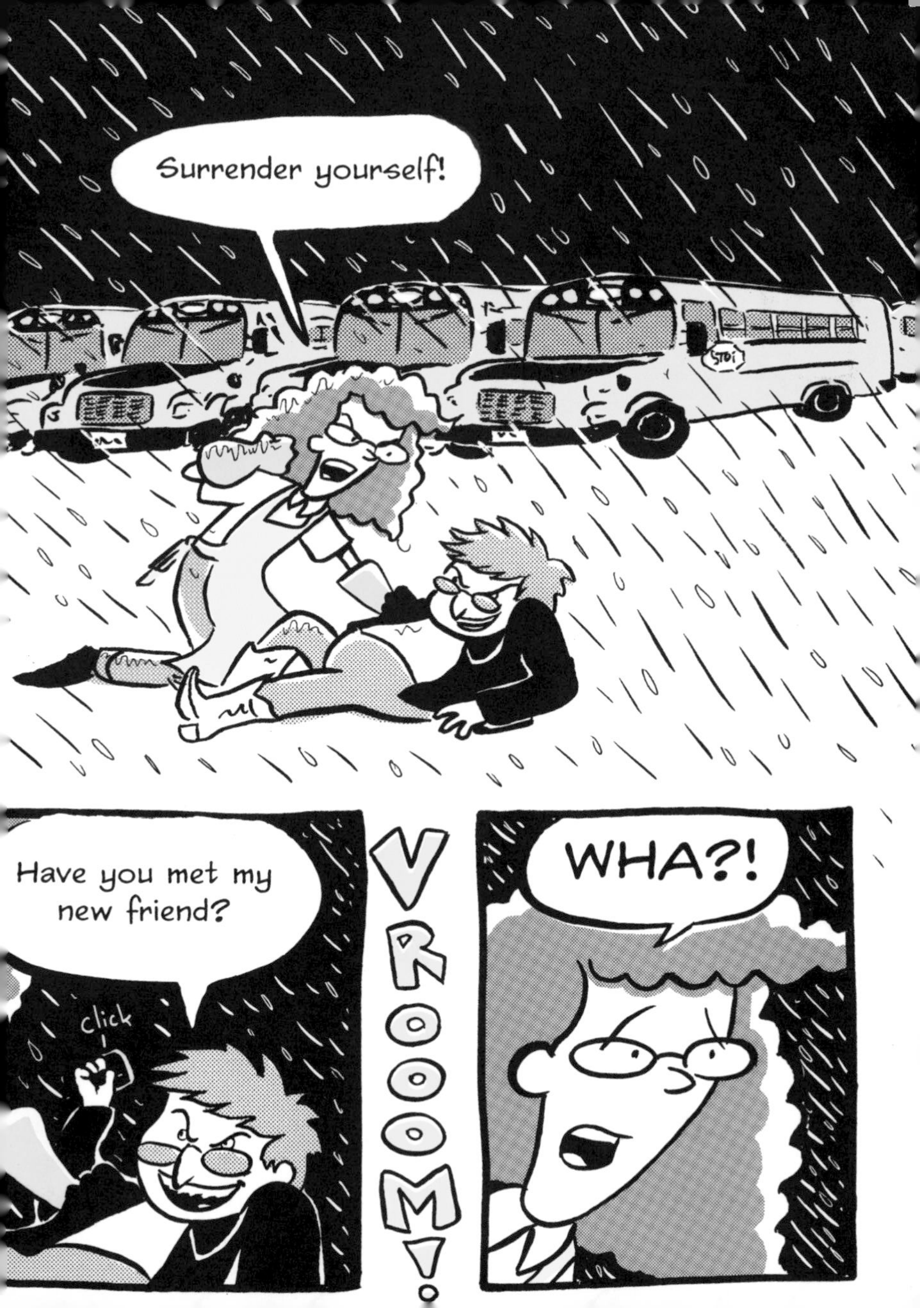
Surrender yourself!
STOP
Have you met my new friend?
click
VROOOOM!
WHA?!

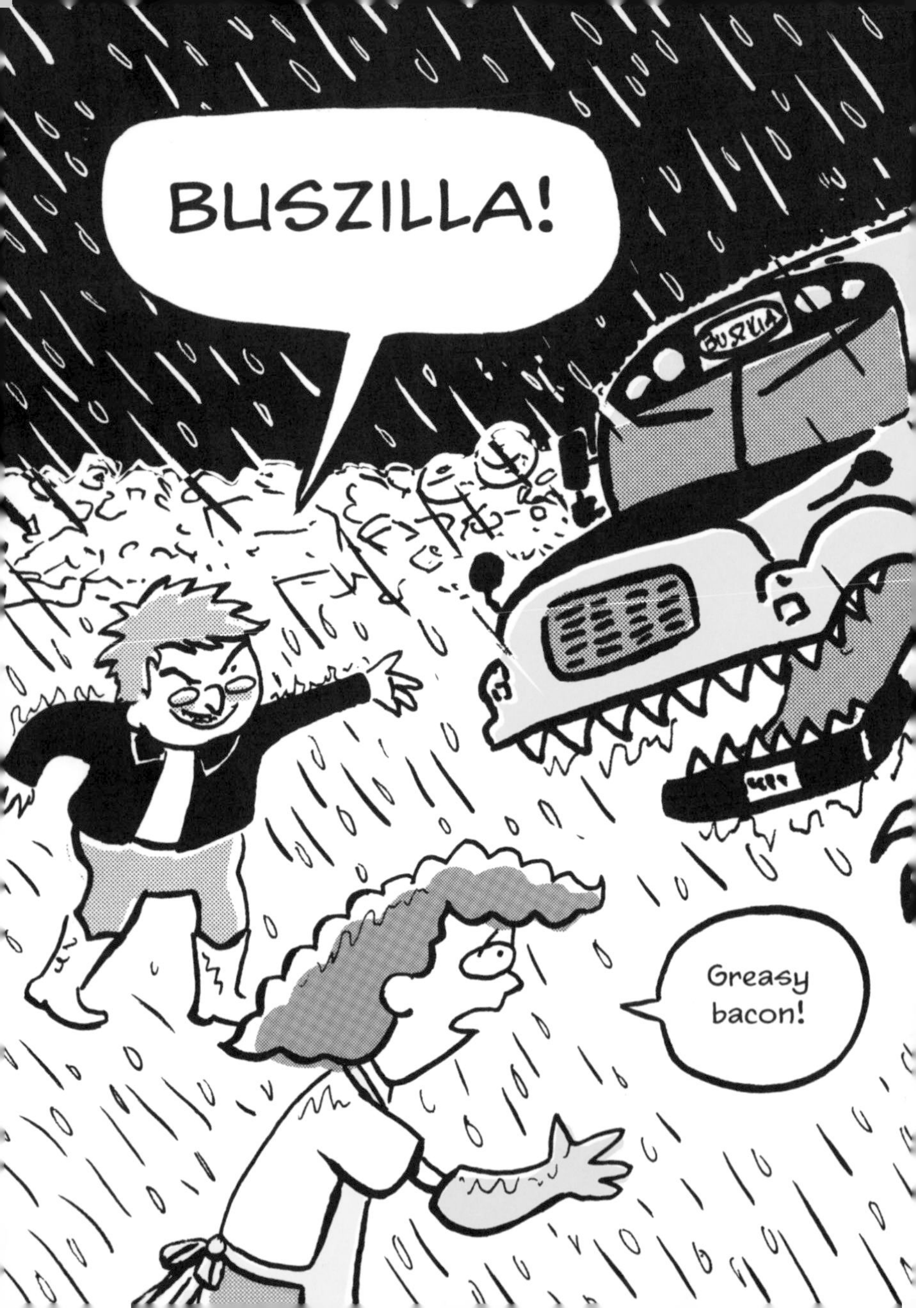
BUSZILLA!
Greasy bacon!

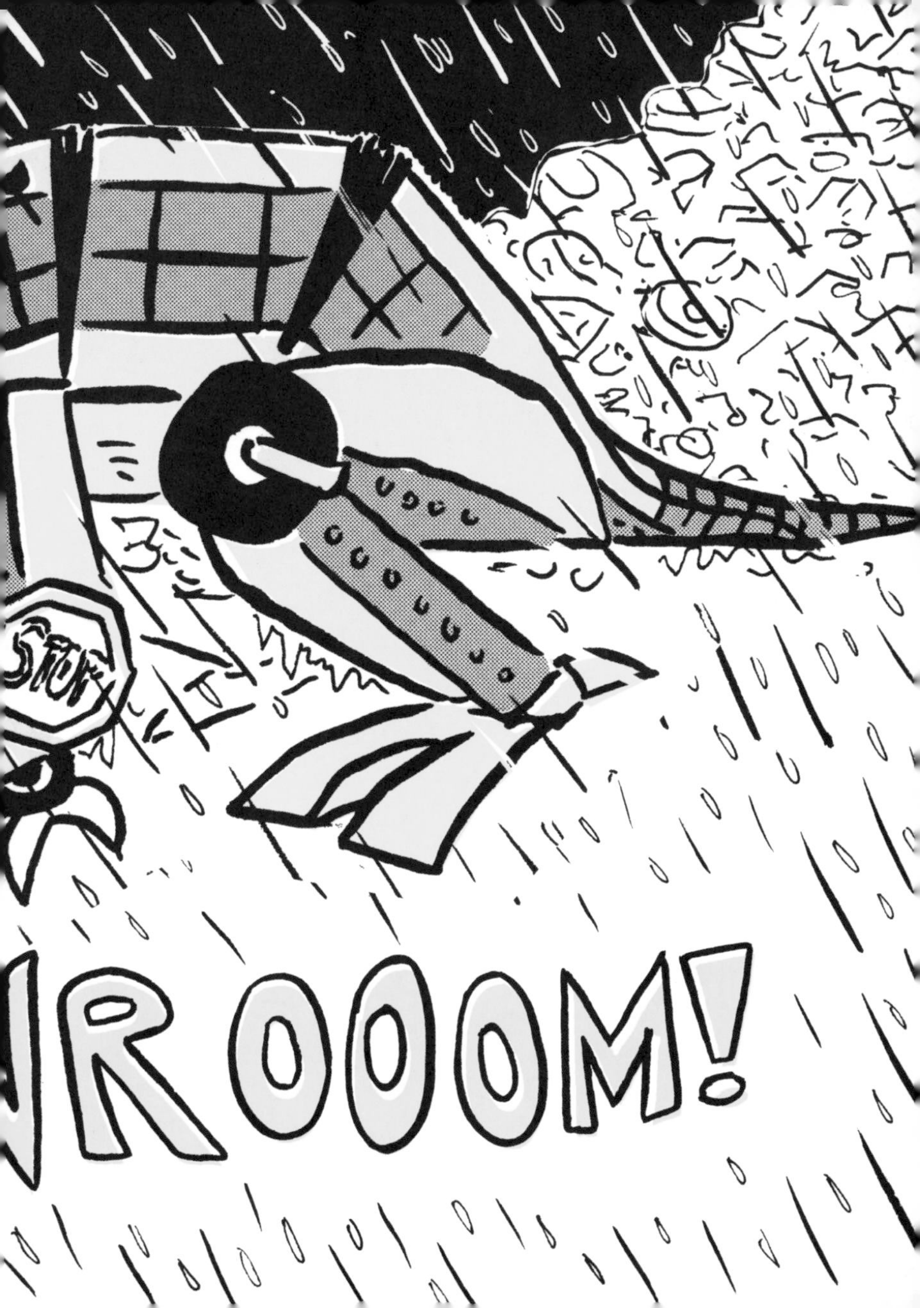
ROOOM!

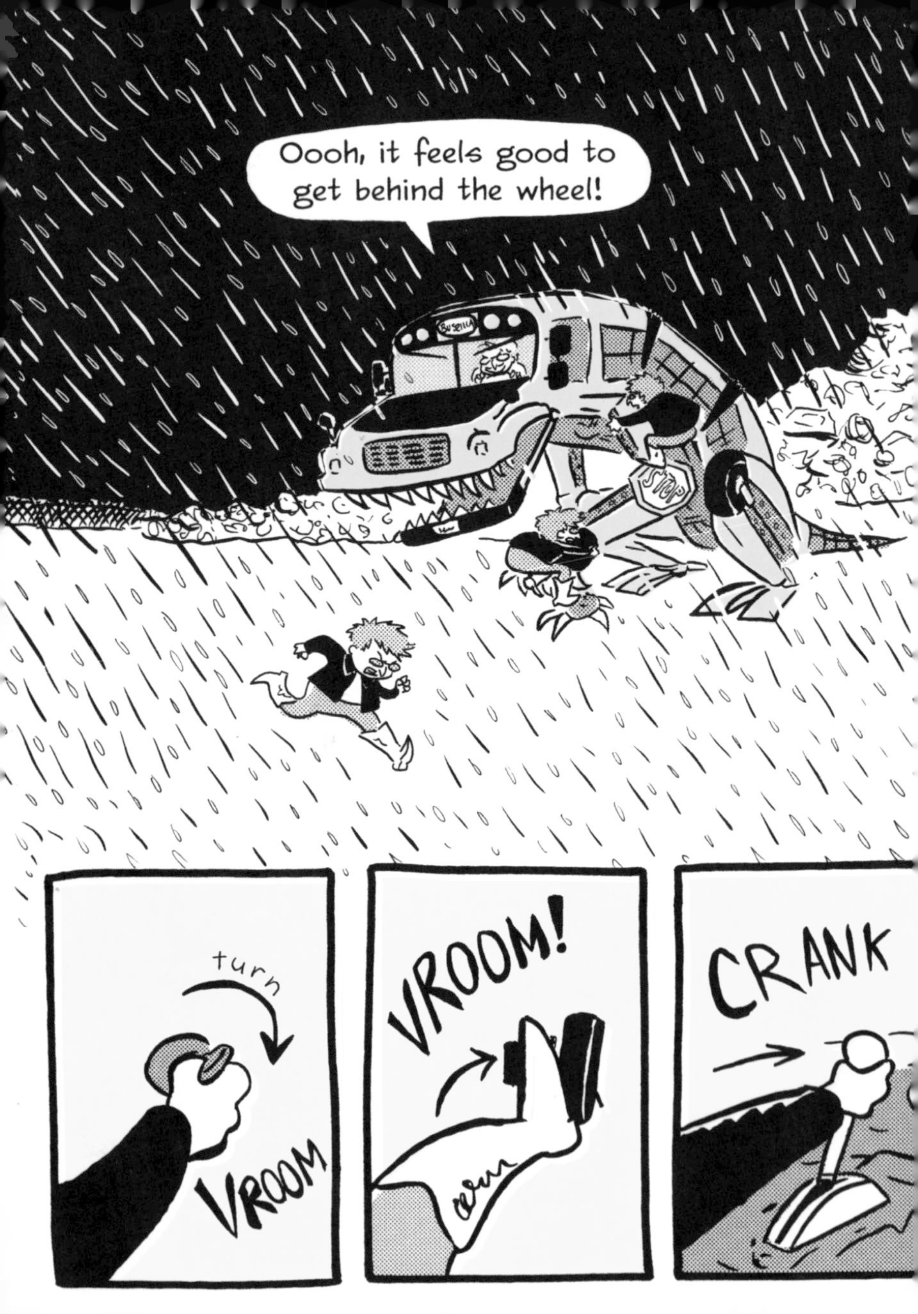
Oooh, it feels good to get behind the wheel!
turn
VROOM
VROOM!
CRANK

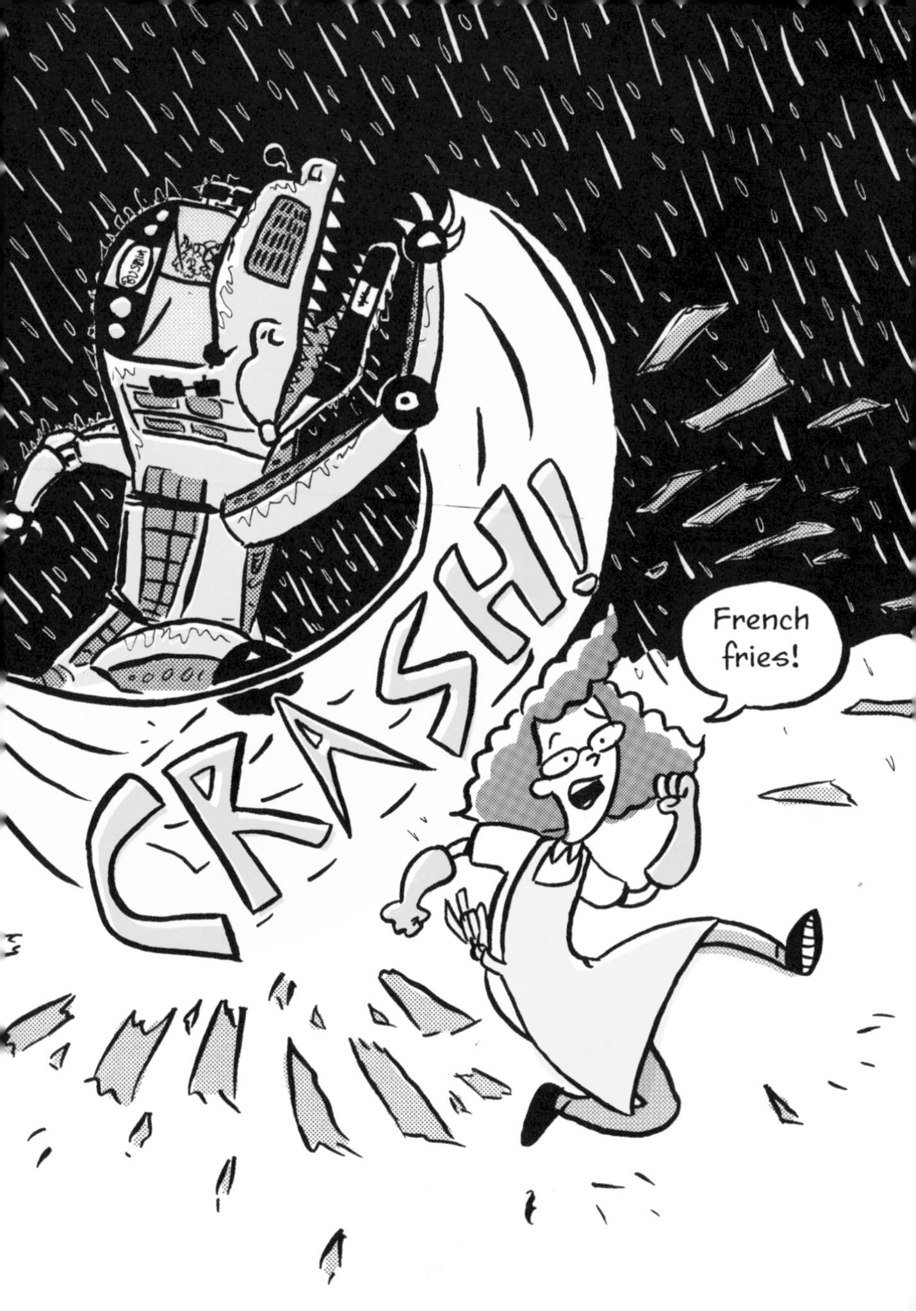
CRASH!!
French fries!

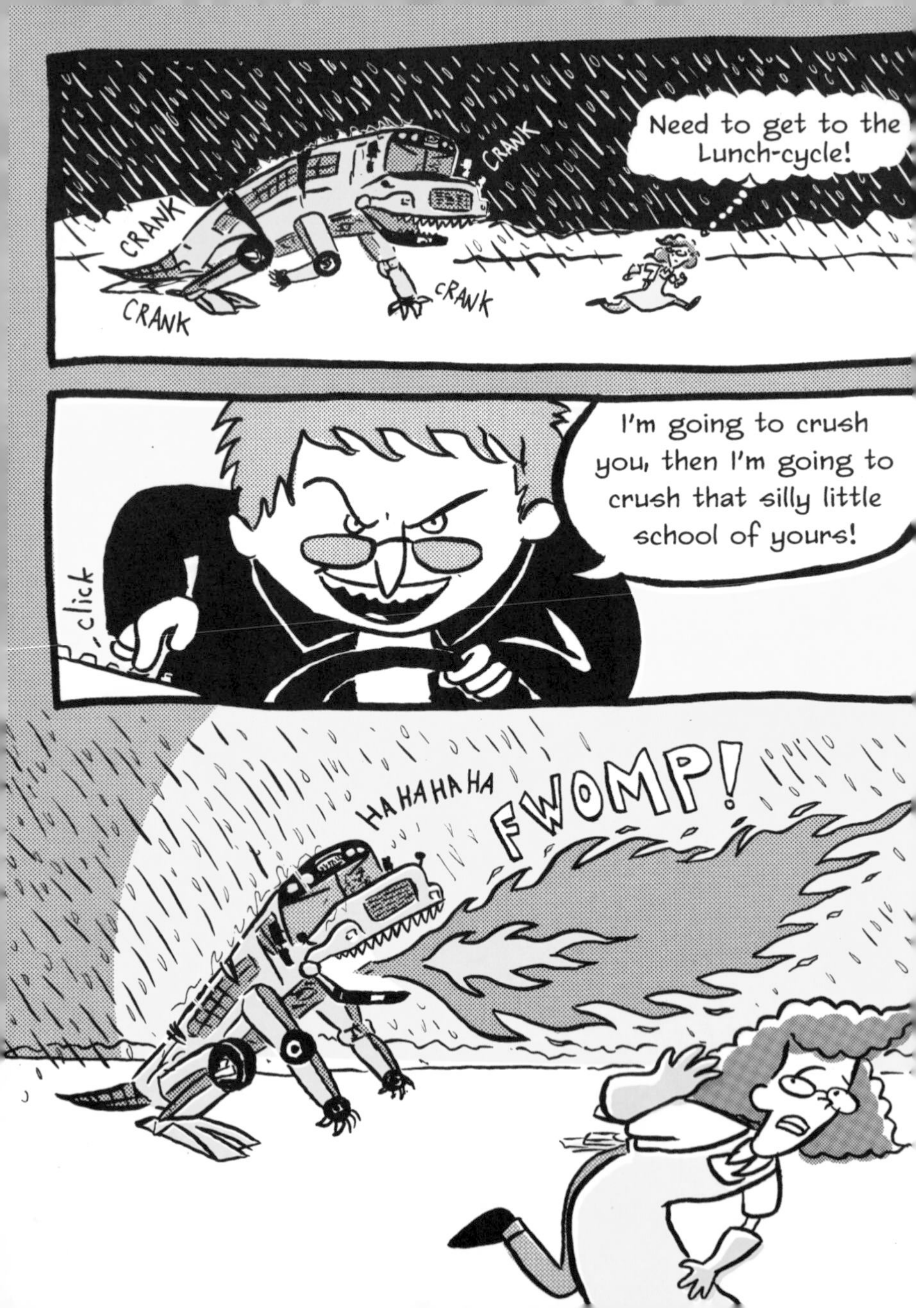

CRANK
CRANK
CRANK
CRANK
Need to get to the Lunch-cycle!
I'm going to crush you, then I'm going to crush that silly little school of yours!
click
HAHAHAHAHA
FWOMP!

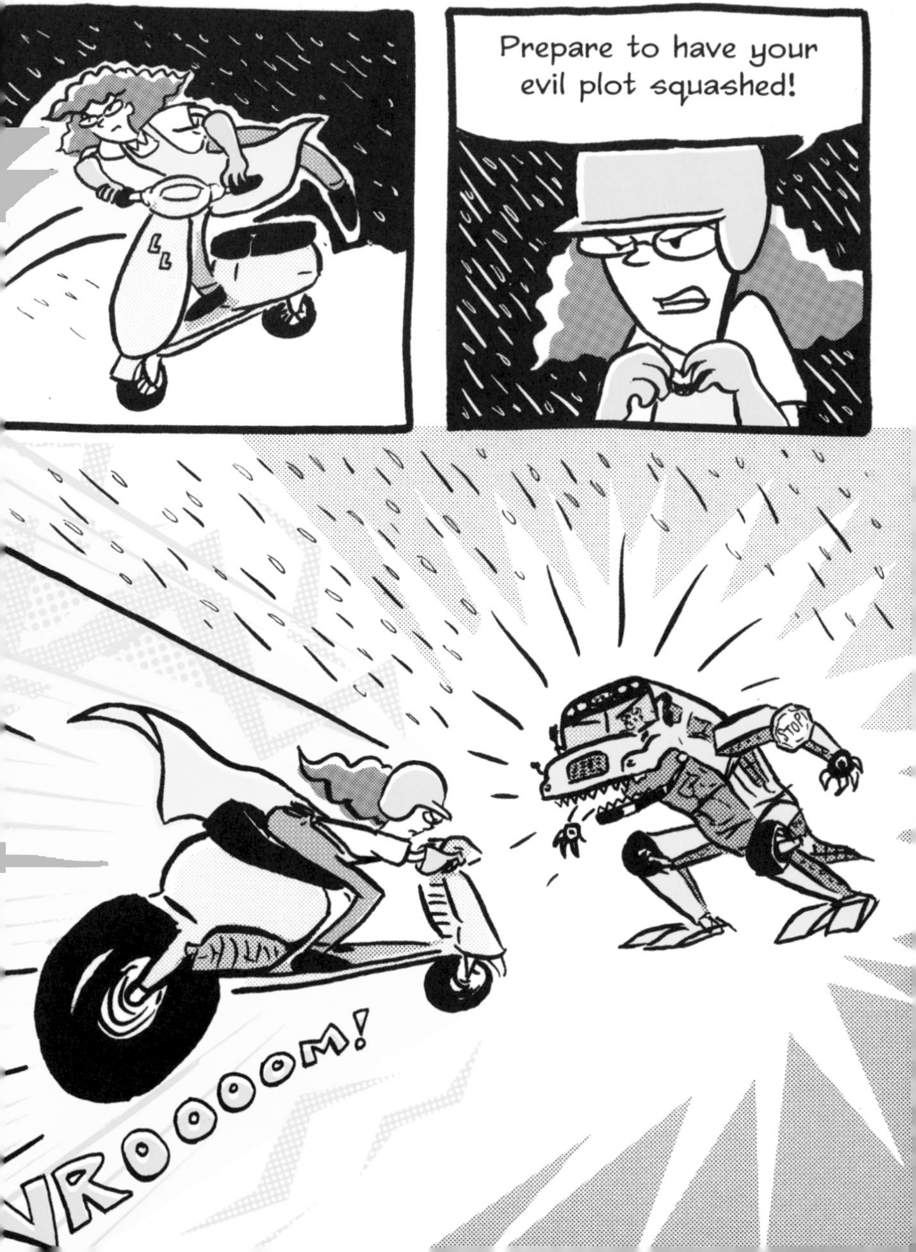
Prepare to have your evil plot squashed!
STOP
VROOOOOM!

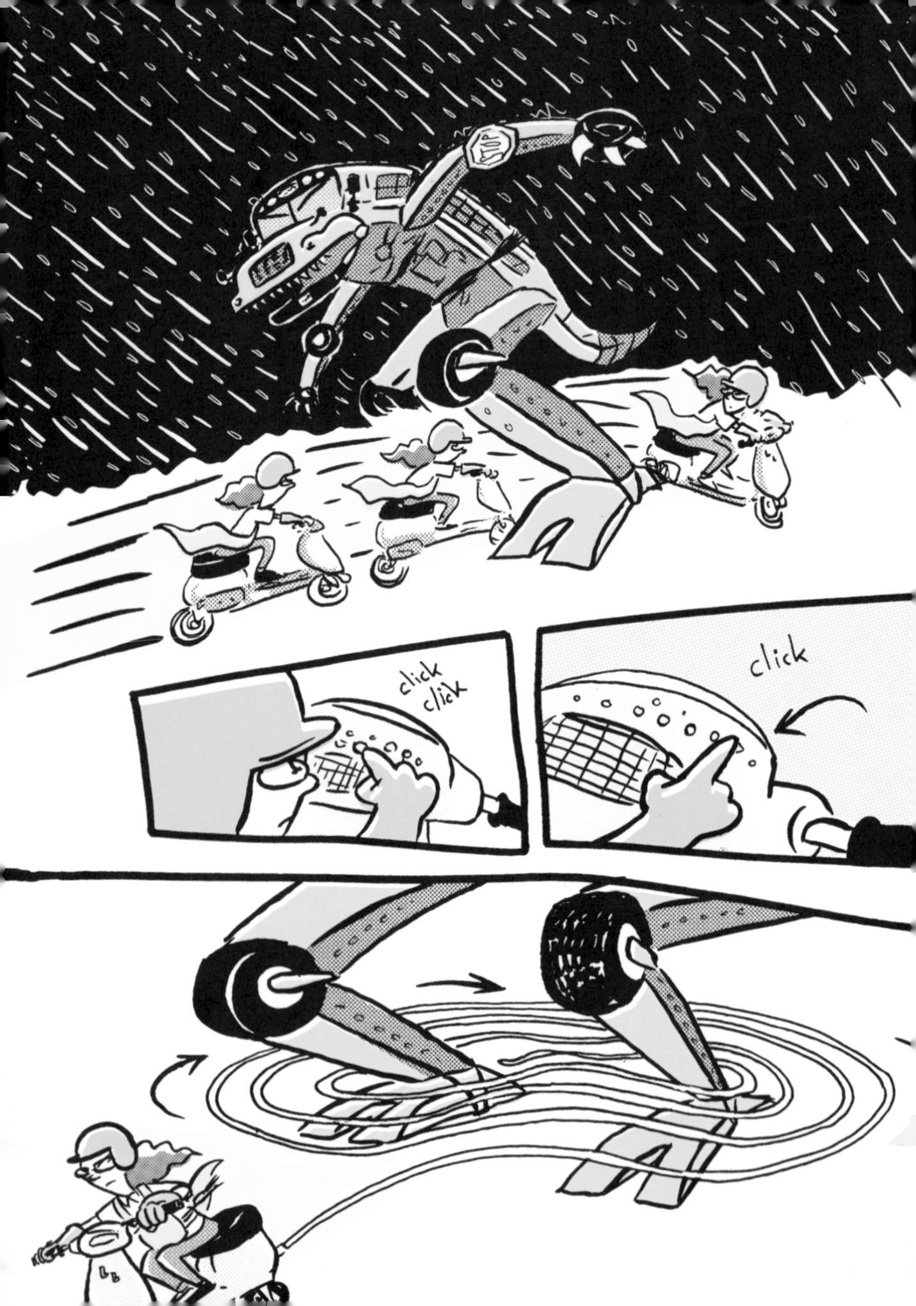
STOP
click
click
click

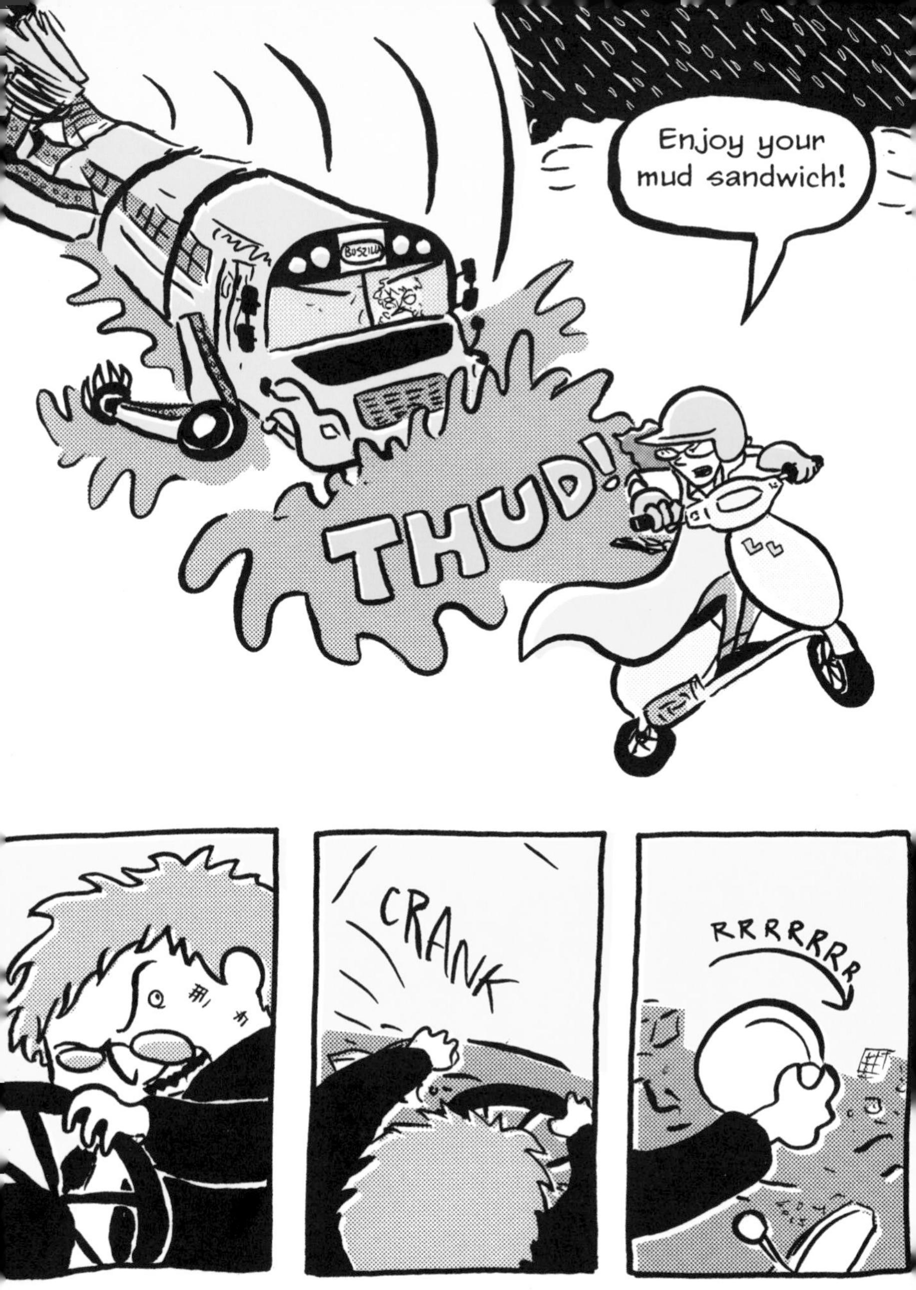
BUSZILLA
Enjoy your mud sandwich!
THUD!
CRANK
RRRRRRRR

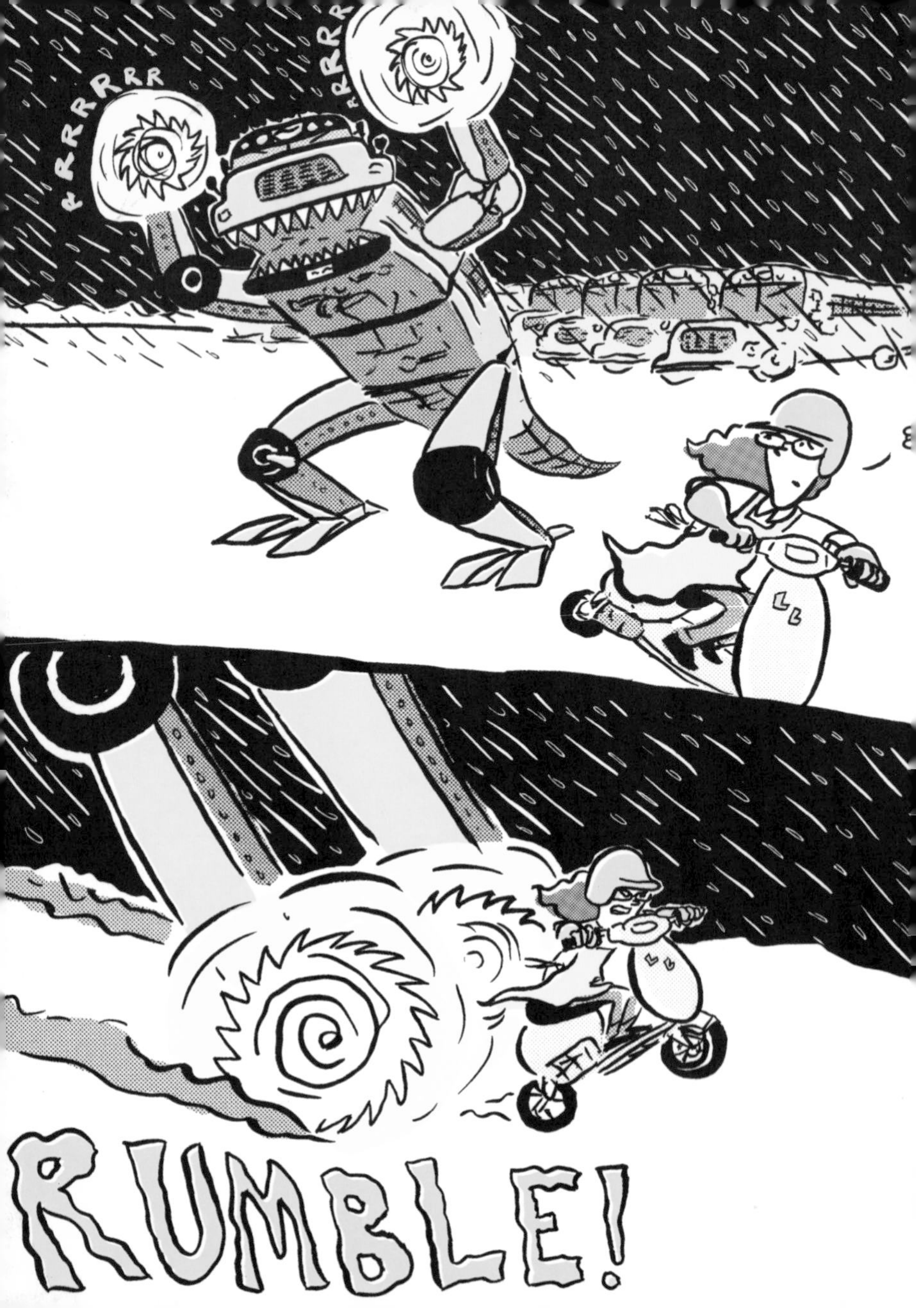
RRRRRRR
RRRRR
RUMBLE!

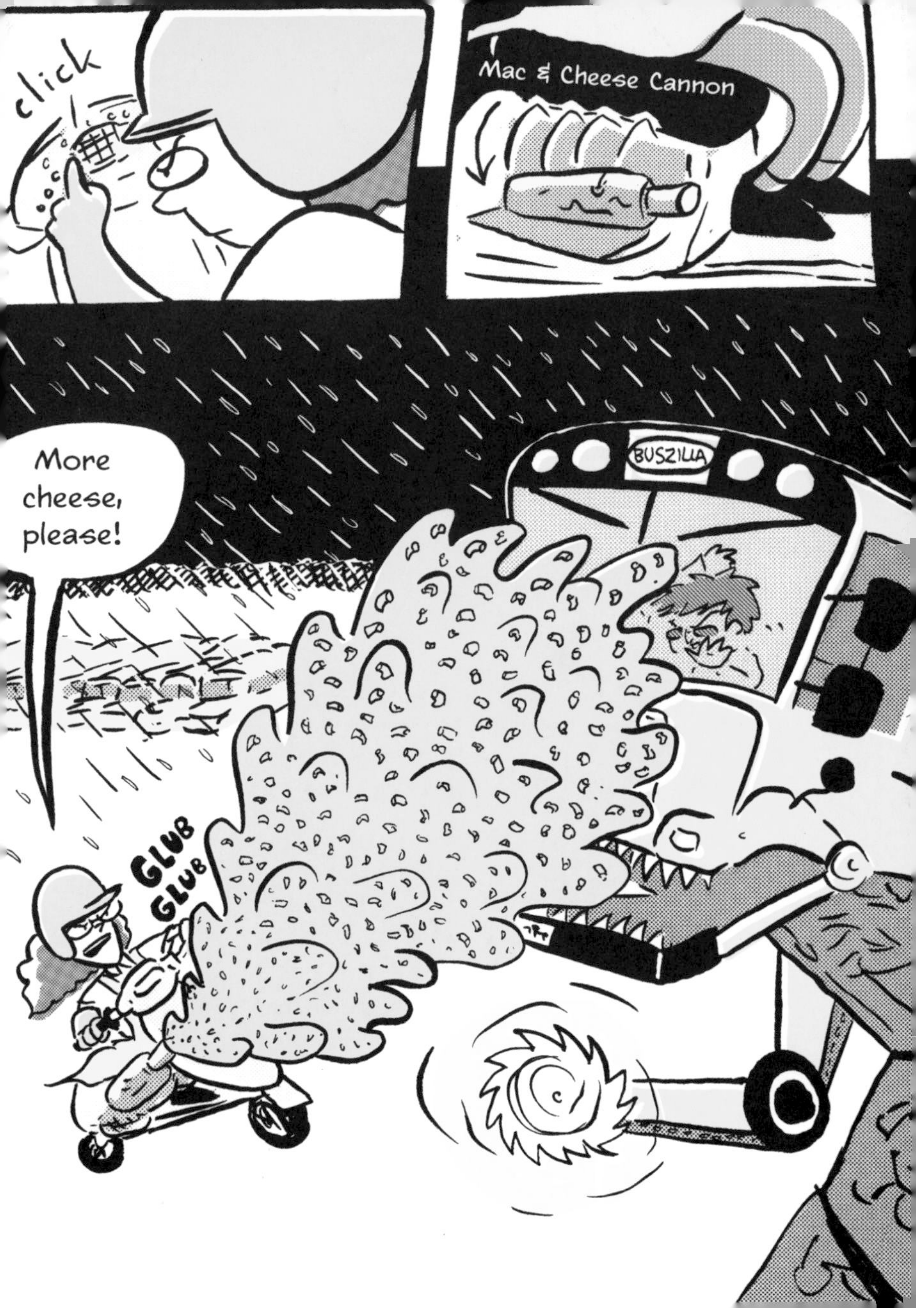
click
Mac & Cheese Cannon
More cheese, please!
BUSZILLA
GLUB GLUB

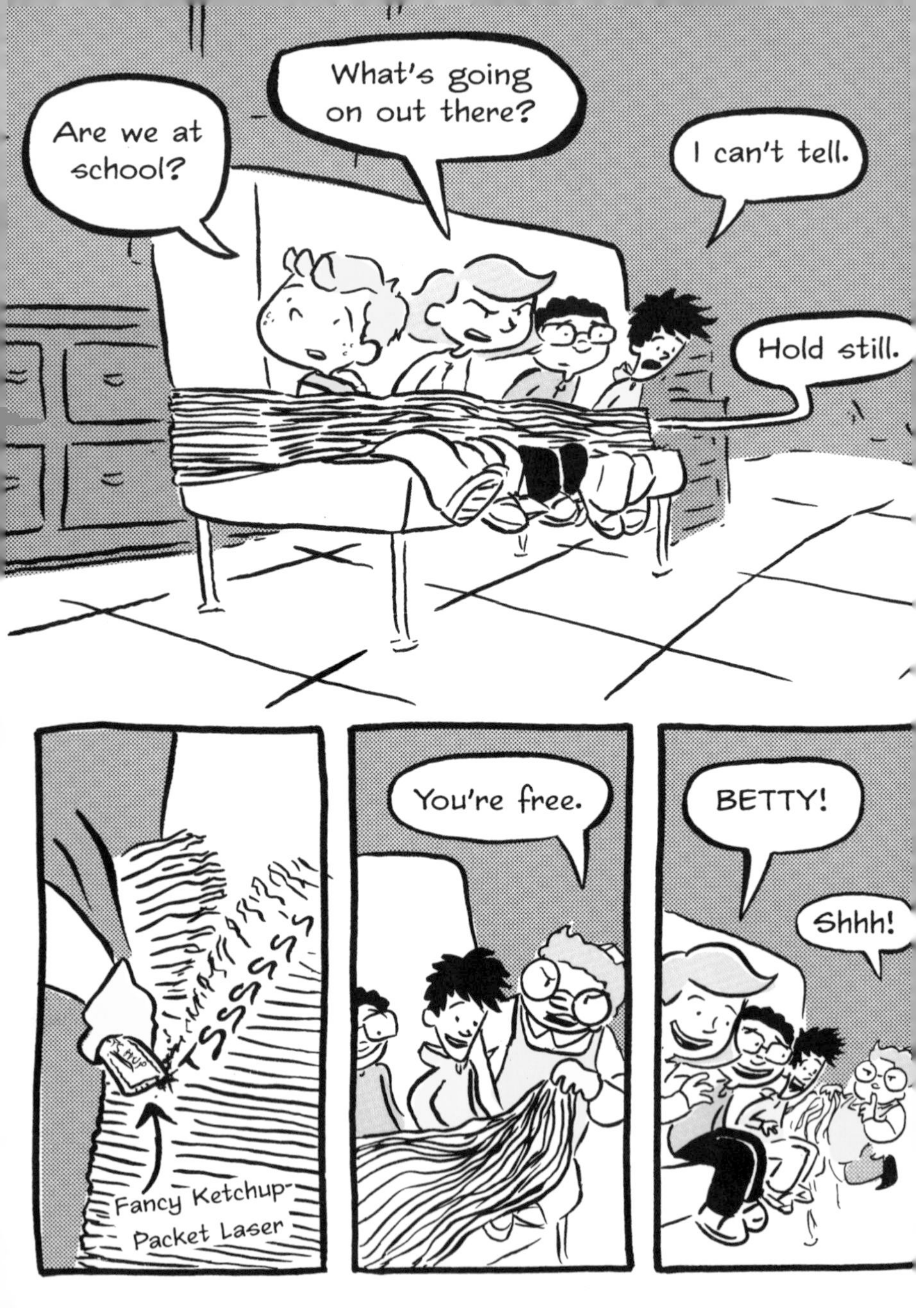
Are we at school?
What's going on out there?
I can't tell.
Hold still.
Fancy Ketchup Packet Laser
TSSSSSS
You're free.
BETTY!
Shhh!

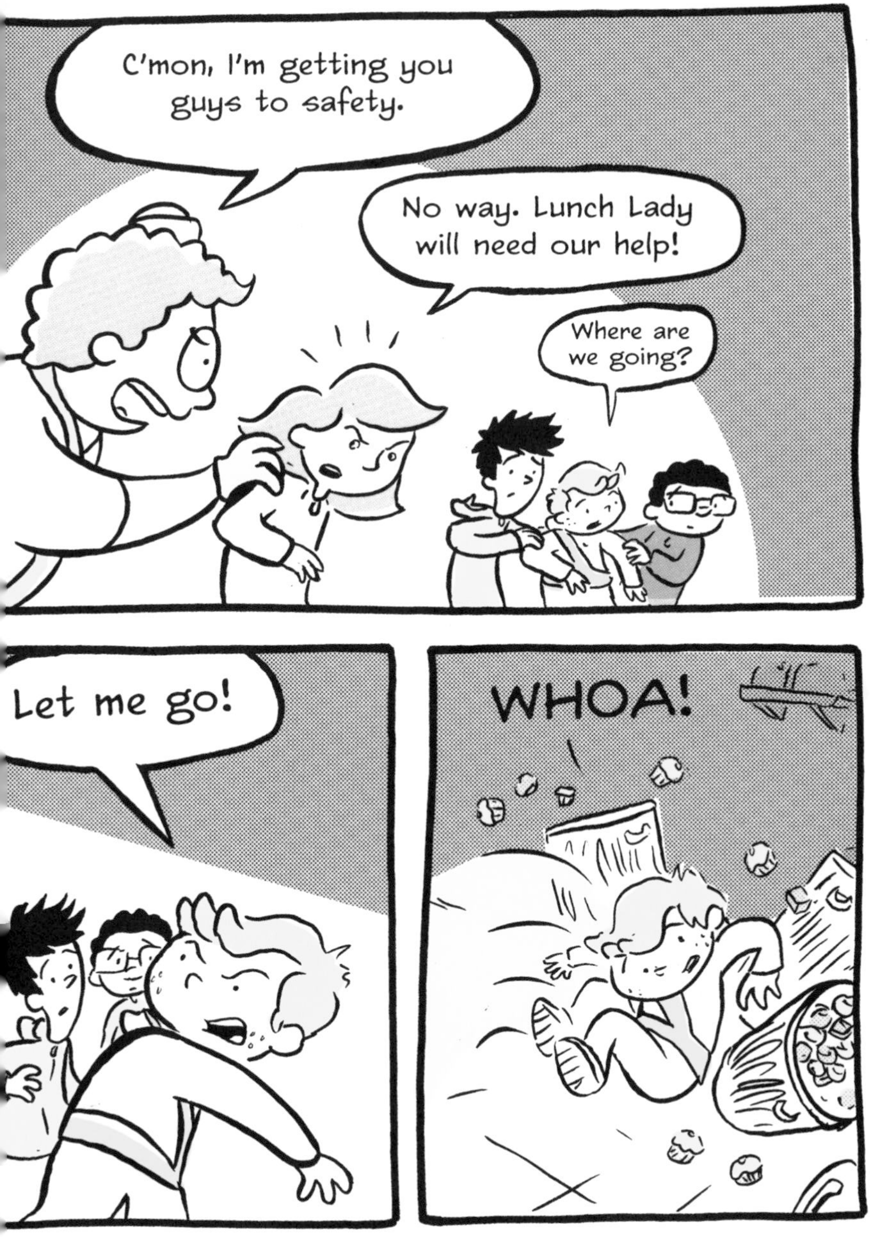
C'mon, I'm getting you guys to safety.
No way. Lunch Lady will need our help!
Where are we going?
Let me go!
WHOA!

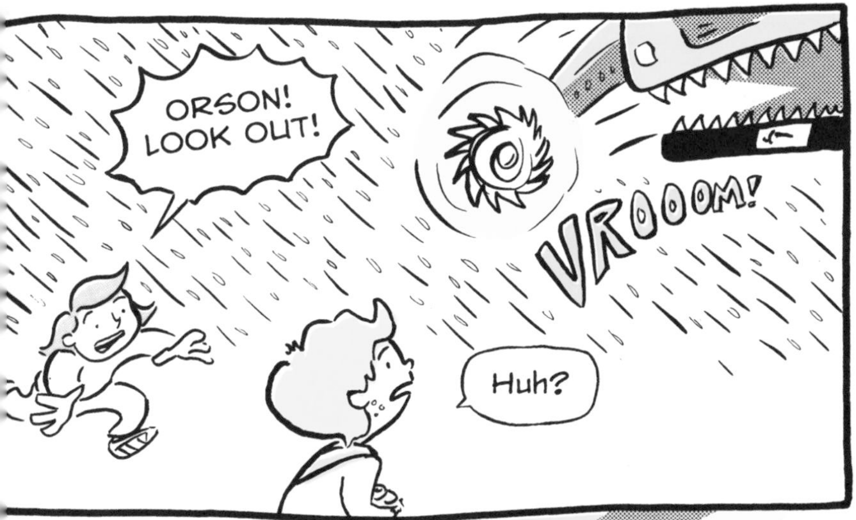
ORSON! LOOK OUT!
VROOOM!
Huh?

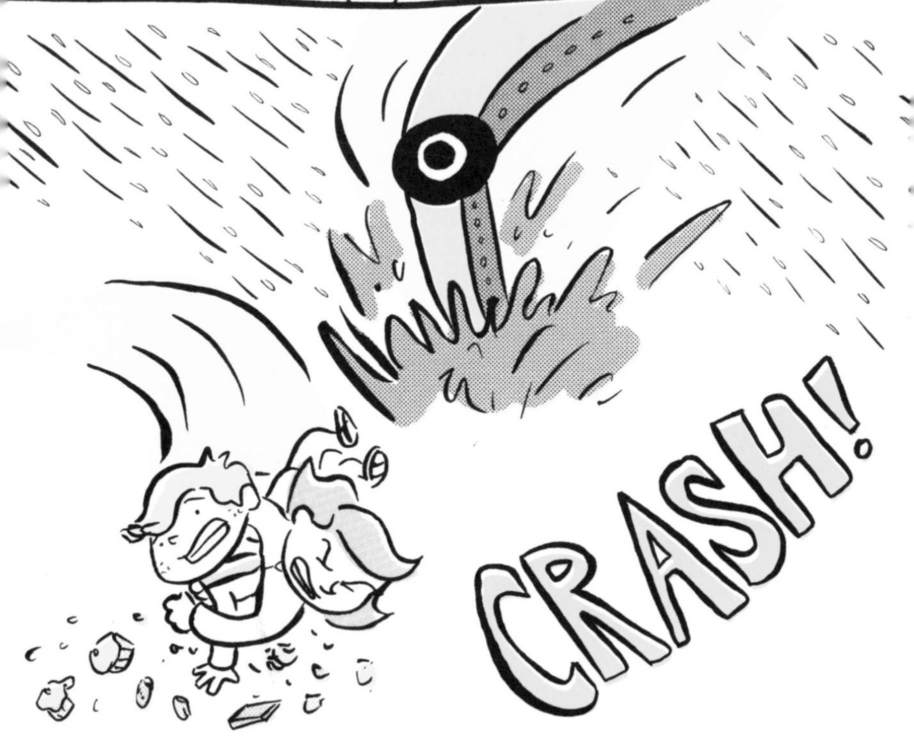
CRASH!

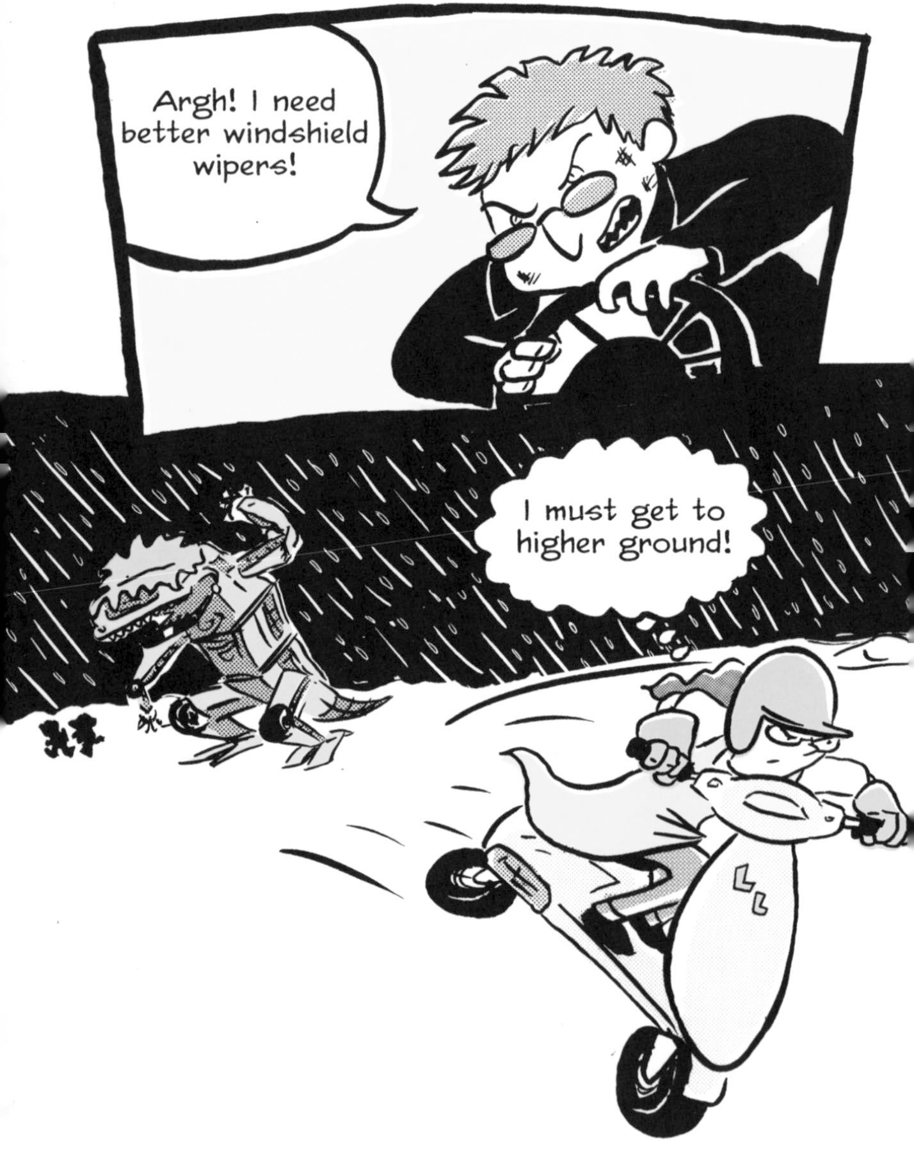
Argh! I need better windshield wipers!
I must get to higher ground!

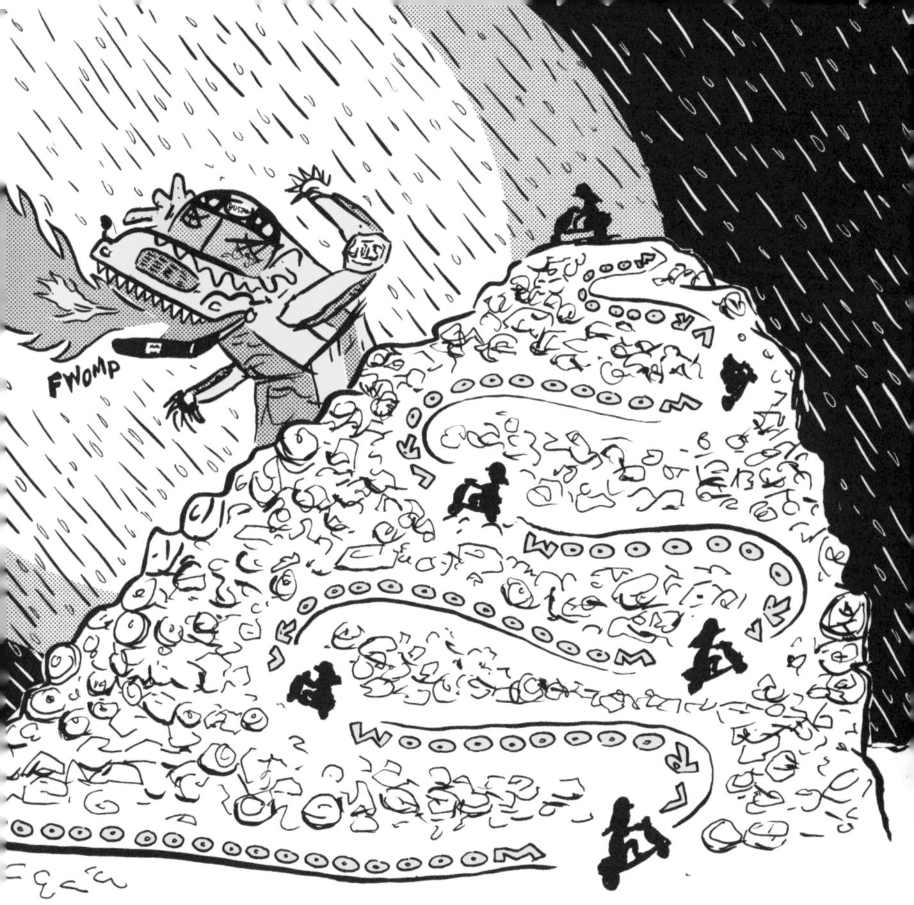
FWOMP

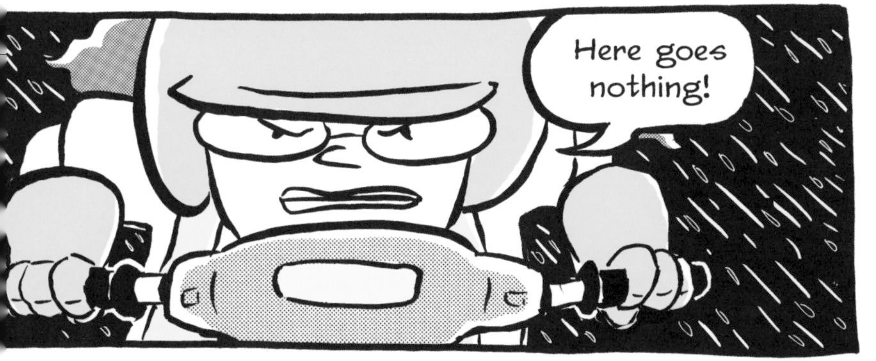
Here goes nothing!

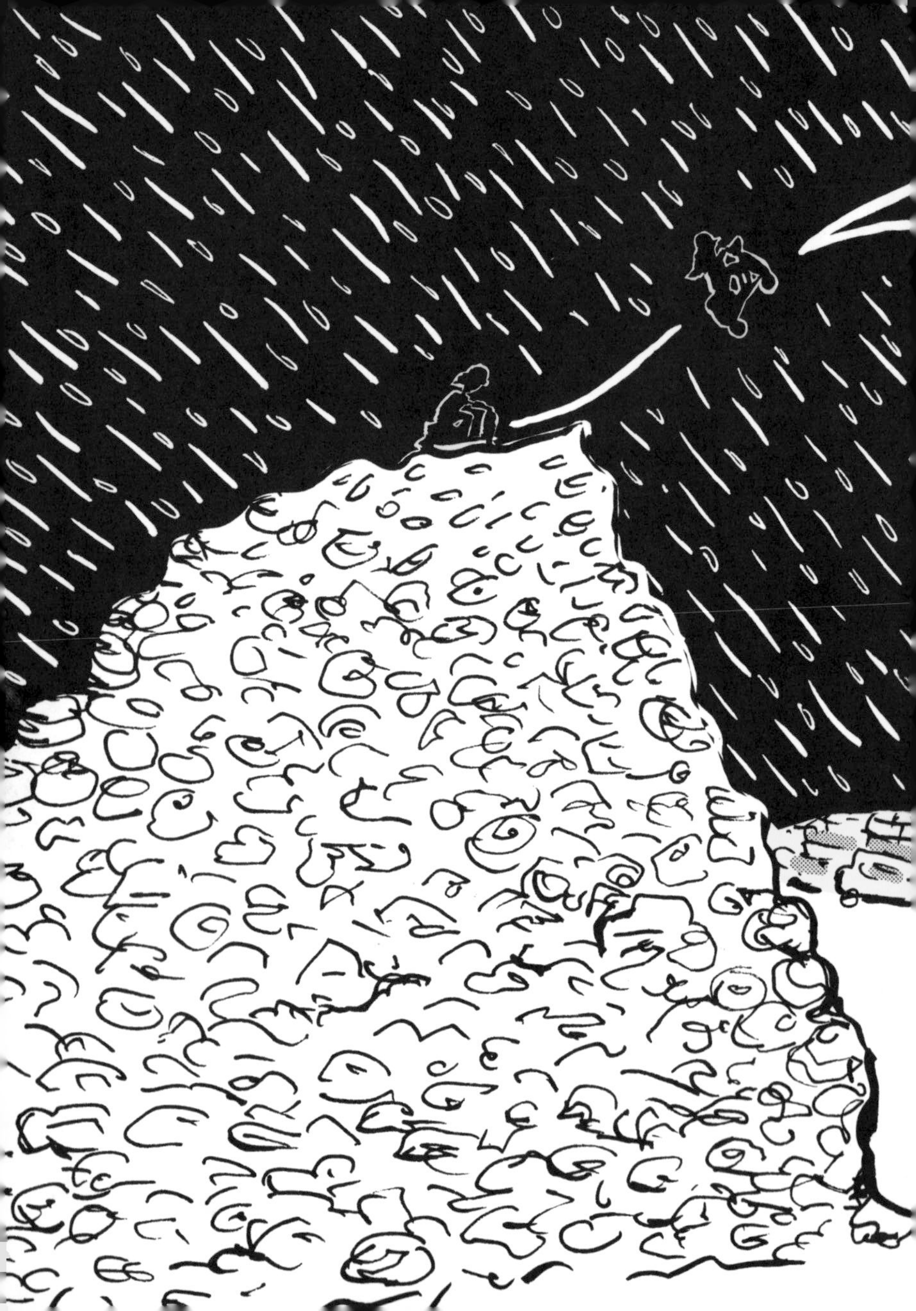

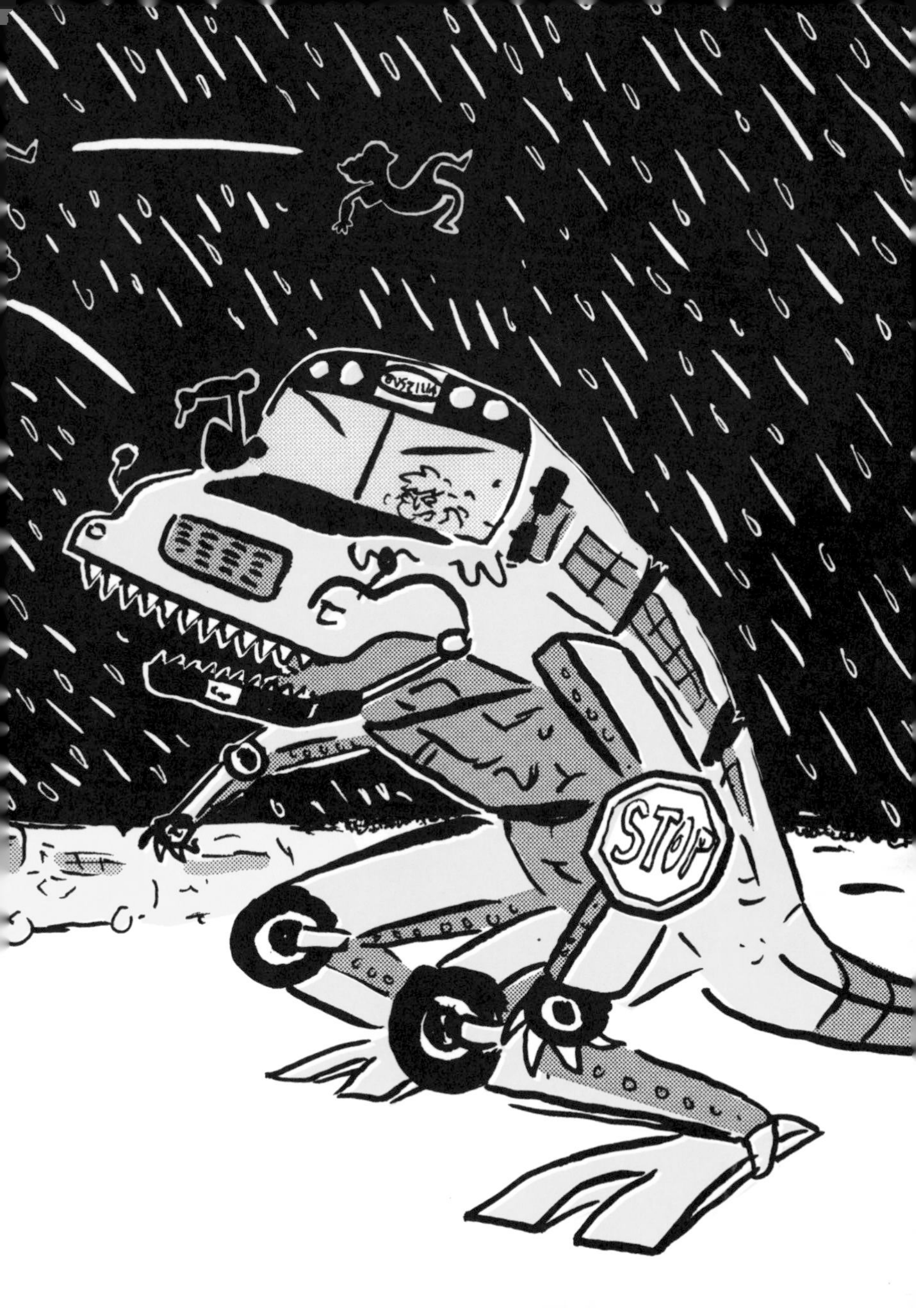
STOP

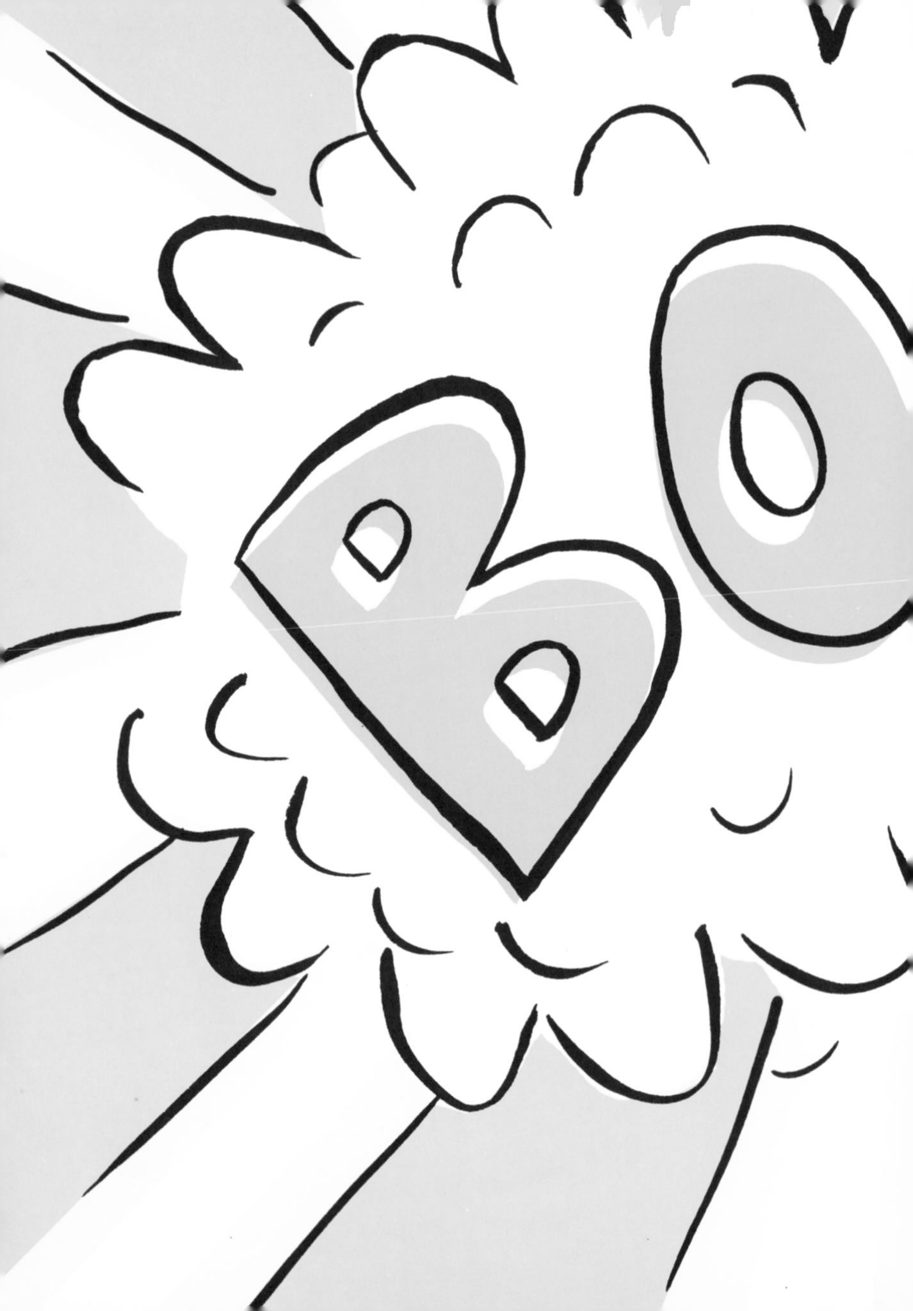
BO

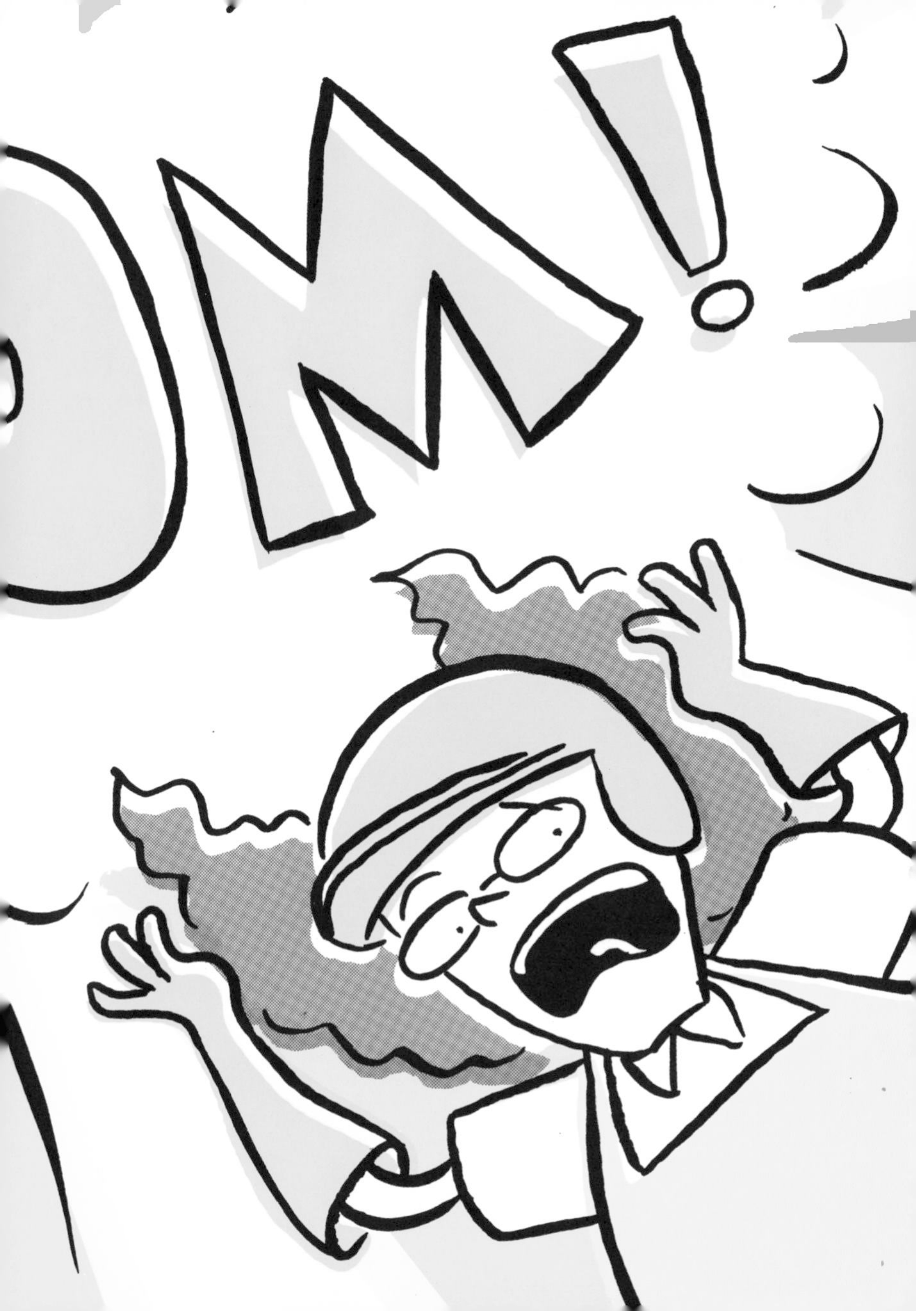
OM!

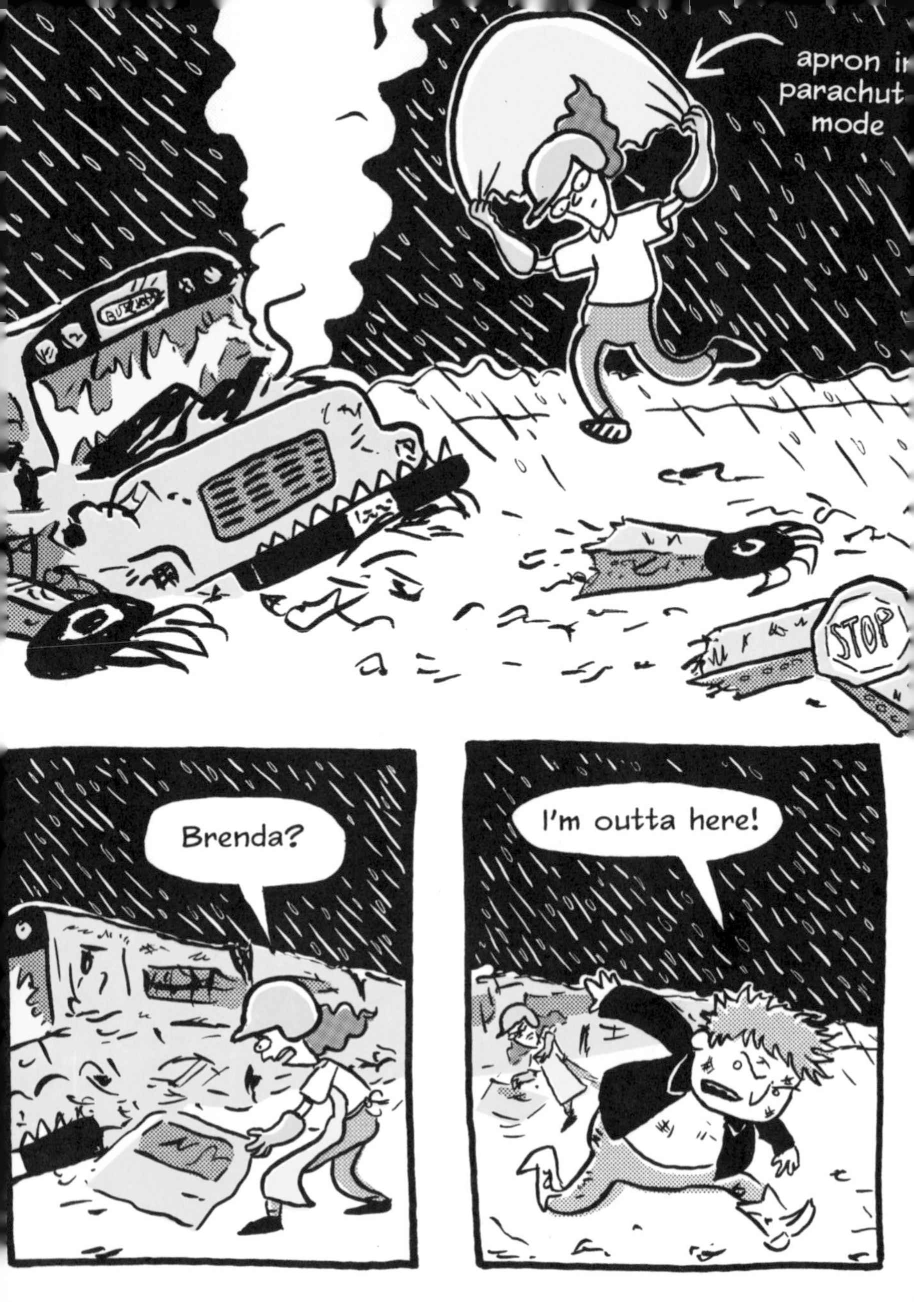
apron i
parachut
mode
STOP
Brenda?
I'm outta here!

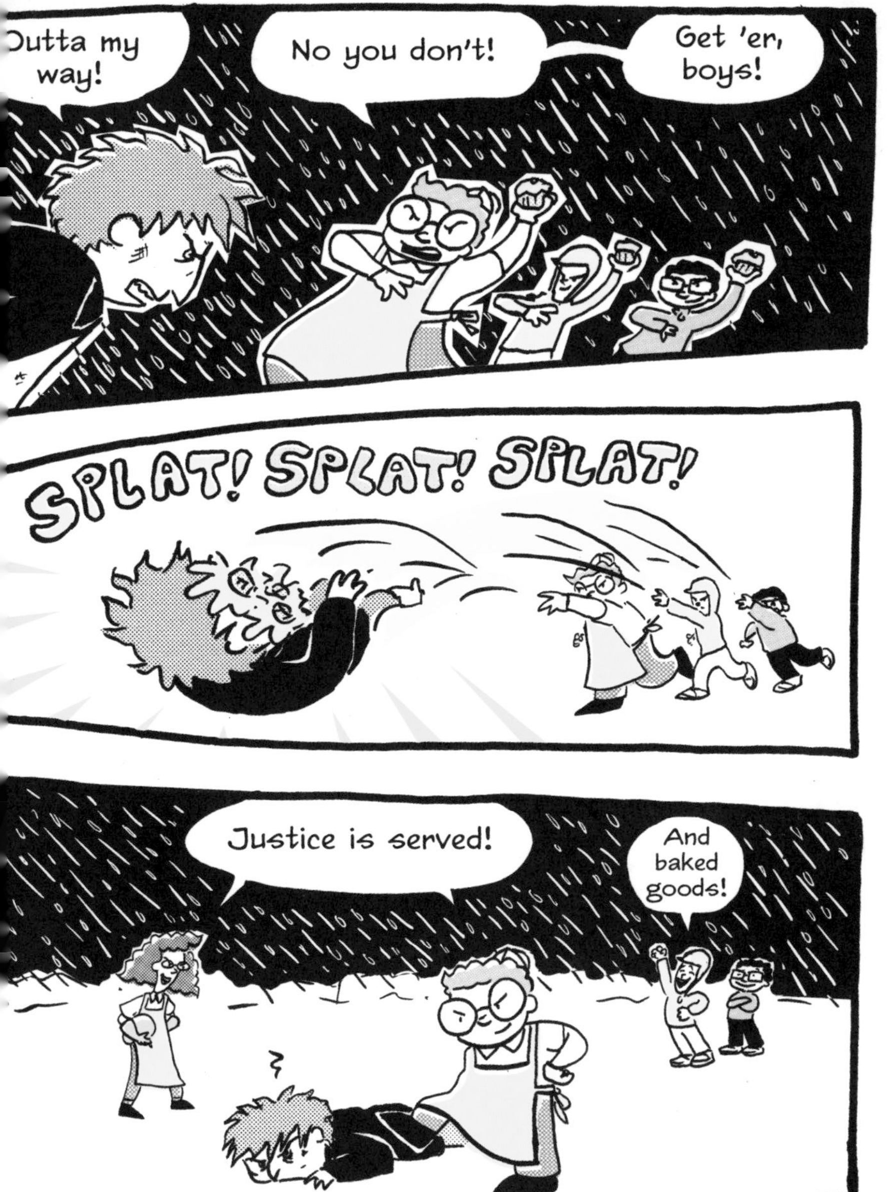
Outta my way!
No you don't!
Get 'er, boys!
SPLAT! SPLAT! SPLAT!
Justice is served!
And baked goods!

The next day at the bake sale . . .

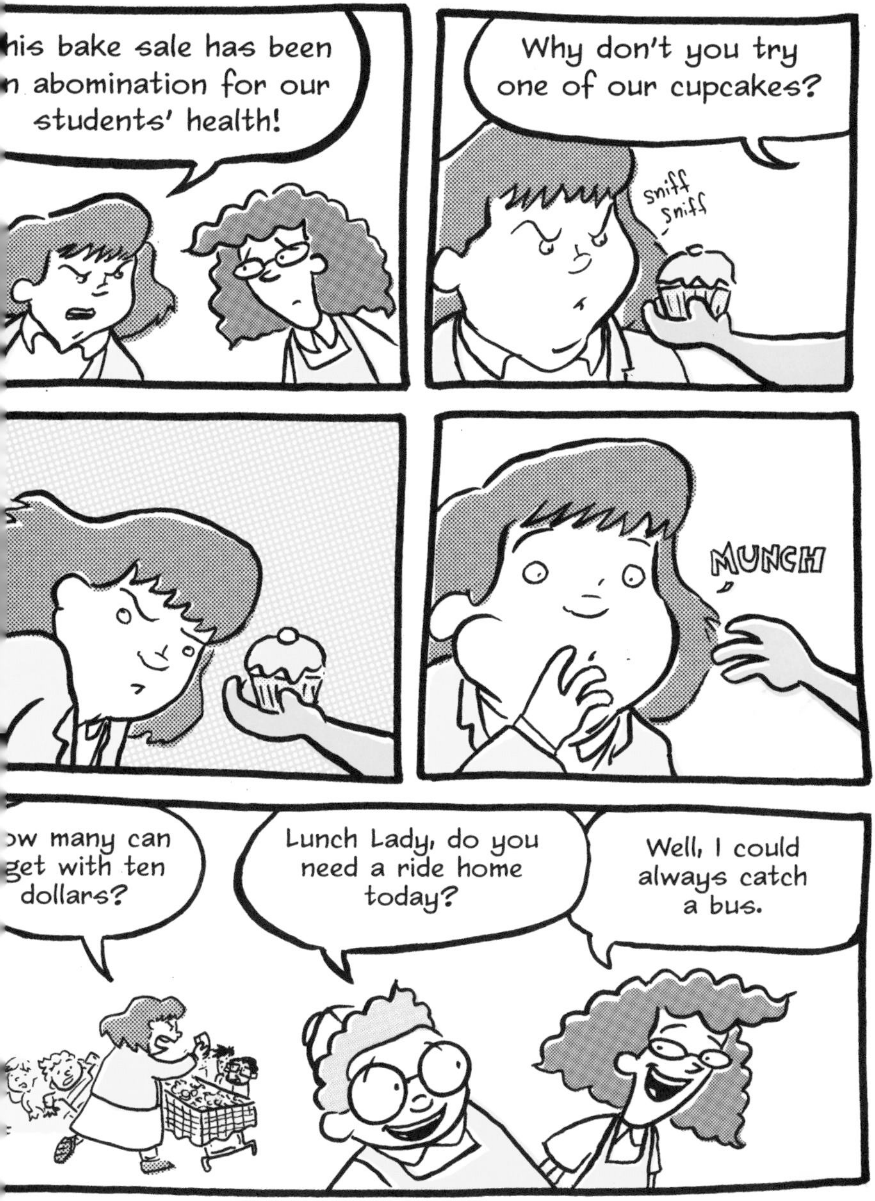
his bake sale has been
n abomination for our
students' health!
Why don't you try
one of our cupcakes?
sniff
sniff
MUNCH
ow many can
get with ten
dollars?
Lunch Lady, do you
need a ride home
today?
Well, I could
always catch
a bus.

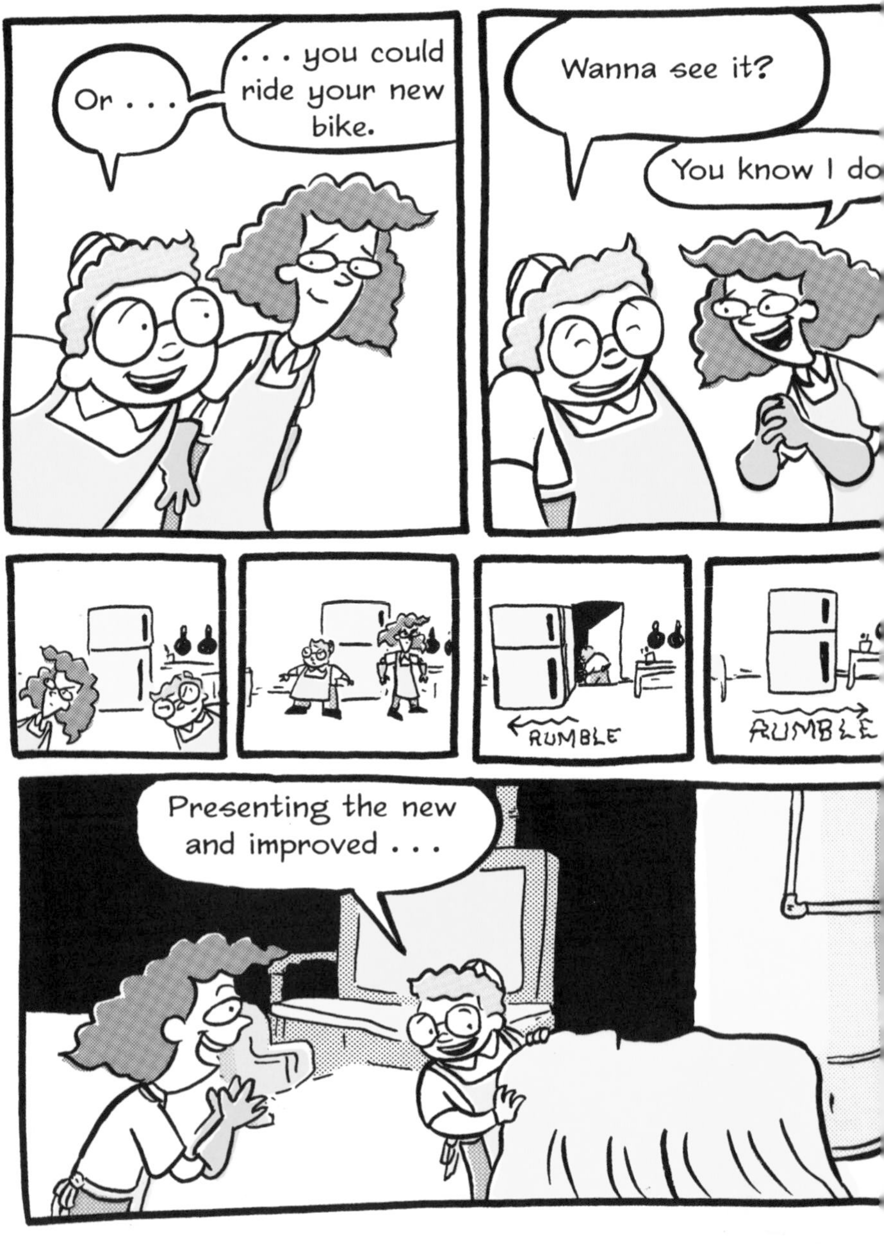

Or . . .
. . . you could ride your new bike.
Wanna see it?
You know I do
RUMBLE
RUMBLE
Presenting the new and improved . . .

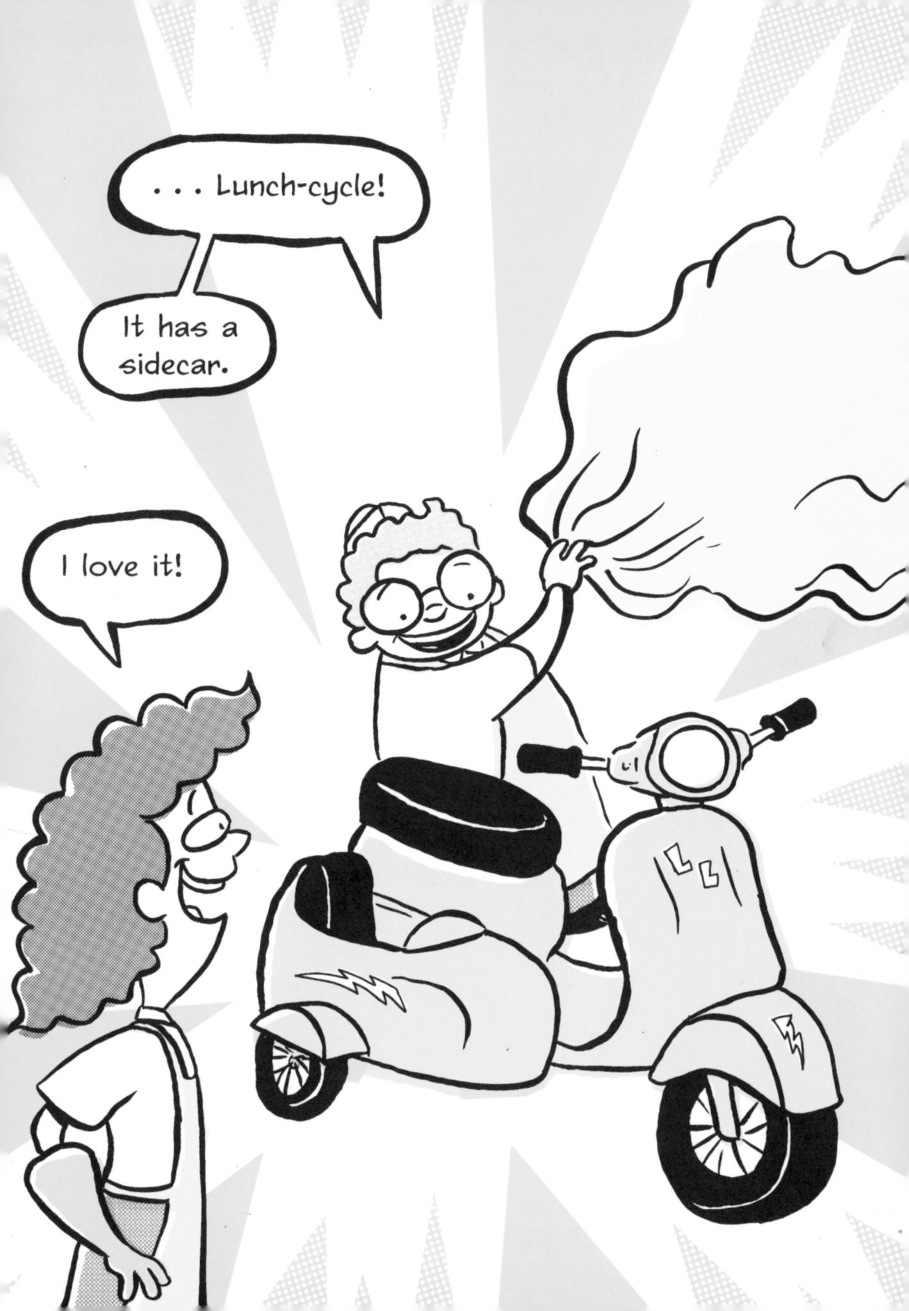
. . . Lunch-cycle!
It has a sidecar.
I love it!

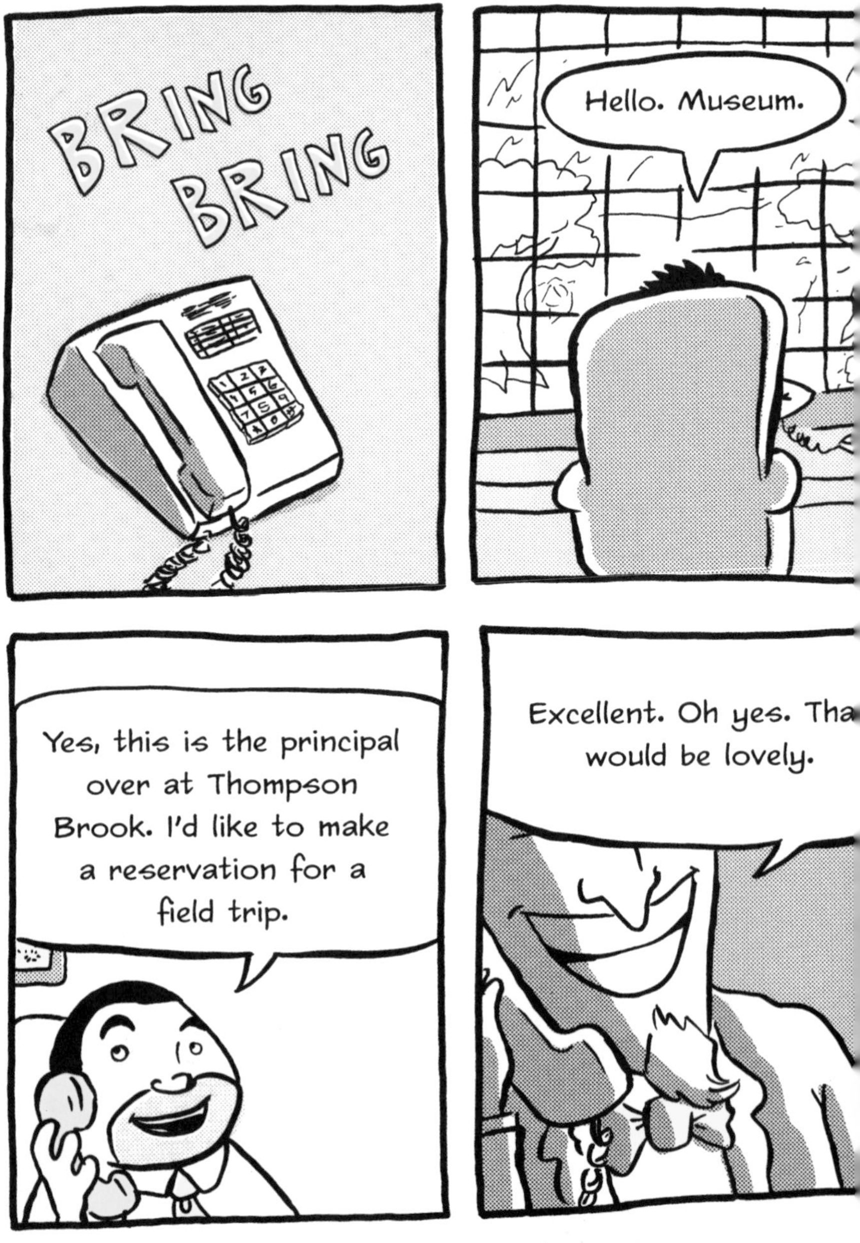
BRING BRING
Hello. Museum.
Yes, this is the principal over at Thompson Brook. I'd like to make a reservation for a field trip.
Excellent. Oh yes. Tha would be lovely.

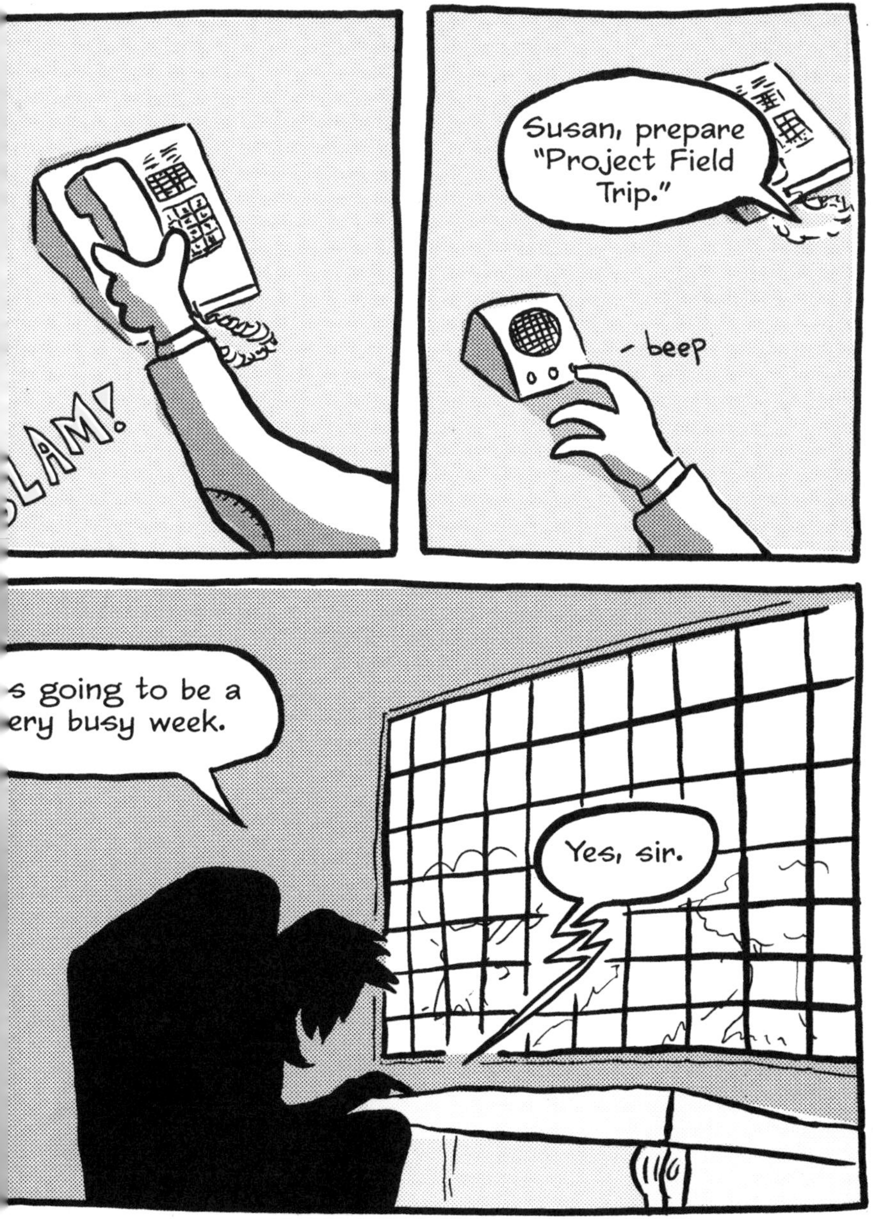
SLAM!
Susan, prepare "Project Field Trip."
- beep
s going to be a ery busy week.
Yes, sir.

FOR RICH AND DAWN
–J.J.K.

The author would like to acknowledge the color assist in this book by Joey Weiser. •

THIS IS A BORZOI BOOK PUBLISHED BY ALFRED A. KNOPF

Visit us on the Web! www.randomhouse.com/kids

Educators and librarians, for a variety of teaching tools,
visit us at www.randomhouse.com/teachers

Library of Congress Cataloging-in-Publication Data
Krosoczka, Jarrett J.
Lunch Lady and the bake sale bandit / Jarrett J. Krosoczka. — 1st ed.
p. cm.
Summary: Lunch Lady, Betty, and the Breakfast Bunch must figure out who is stealing the goods from the bake sale.
ISBN 978-0-375-86729-3 (trade pbk.) — ISBN 978-0-375-96729-0 (lib. bdg.)
1. Graphic novels. [1. Graphic novels. 2. School lunchrooms, cafeterias, etc.—Fiction.
3. Stealing—Fiction. 4. Schools—Fiction. 5. Mystery and detective stories.] I. Title.
PZ7.7.K76Ltm 2010
[Fic]—dc22
2010012781

The text of this book is set in Hedge Backwards.
The illustrations in this book were created using ink on paper and digital coloring.

MANUFACTURED IN MALAYSIA
December 2010
10 9 8 7 6 5 4 3 2

First Edition

JOSEPHUS

COMPLETE WORKS

Includes:

LIFE OF FLAVIUS JOSEPHUS
THE ANTIQUITIES OF THE JEWS
THE WARS OF THE JEWS
DISCOURSE CONCERNING HADES
SEVEN DISSERTATIONS
TABLES OF JEWISH WEIGHTS AND MEASURES
LIST OF ANCIENT TESTIMONIES AND RECORDS CITED BY JOSEPHUS
TEXTS OF THE OLD TESTAMENT PARALLEL TO JOSEPHUS' HISTORIES

20 FULL-PAGE ILLUSTRATIONS

TRANSLATED BY WILLIAM WHISTON, A.M.
Foreword by William Sanford LaSor, Ph.D., Th.D.

KREGEL PUBLICATIONS
GRAND RAPIDS, MICHIGAN 49501

Foreword Copyright © 1960
by KREGEL PUBLICATIONS
Library of Congress Catalog
Card Number 60-15405

This new popularly priced edition of the COMPLETE WORKS OF FLAVIUS JOSEPHUS is a combination of the William Whiston translation published by William P. Nimmo, Edinburgh, Scotland in 1867 and the Standard Edition published by Porter and Coates, Philadelphia, Pennsylvania.

ISBN 0 - 8254 - 2951 - X (Cloth)
ISBN 0 - 8254 - 2952 - 8 (Paper)

SECOND PRINTING 1963
THIRD PRINTING 1964
FOURTH PRINTING 1966
FIFTH PRINTING 1967
SIXTH PRINTING 1969
SEVENTH PRINTING 1970
EIGHTH PRINTING 1970
NINTH PRINTING 1971
TENTH PRINTING 1972
ELEVENTH PRINTING 1973
TWELFTH PRINTING 1974
THIRTEENTH PRINTING 1976
FOURTEENTH PRINTING 1977

PRINTED IN THE UNITED STATES OF AMERICA

CONTENTS

CONTENTS

LIST OF ILLUSTRATIONS